FEAR FOR FRANCES

FEAR FOR FRANCES

Veronica Heley

CHIVERS

British Library Cataloguing in Publication Data available

This Large Print edition published by AudioGO Ltd, Bath, 2013.
Published by arrangement with the Author.

U.K. Hardcover   ISBN   978 1 4713 2001 9
U.K. Softcover   ISBN   978 1 4713 2002 6

Printed and bound in Great Britain by
MPG Books Group Limited

CHAPTER ONE

Was there a curse on the house of Broome? The servants certainly thought so, but Miss Frances Chard rejected the idea out of hand. This was 1881, not 1481, and although part of Furze Court had once been an abbey, and still lacked such modern conveniences as gas lighting, that was no excuse, said Miss Chard, for believing in ghosts, curses, or things that went bump in the night.

Agnes Broome believed in them, but Agnes was only thirteen and it was up to Miss Chard, as her governess, to drum some sense into the child.

However, when both Richard and Gavin Broome were brought back to the Court at death's door, and that within three months of her arrival at her post, Miss Chard began to wonder . . .

*   *   *

Richard, 10th Baron Broome, had been a genial fair-headed giant of a man. A hard-drinking spendthrift, he had been carelessly kind to the penniless aunt who acted as hostess for him, and to his younger cousin Agnes, who adored him. He had been engaged to be married to Maud, Agnes's elder sister, when

1

he took a toss on the hunting field, just a week before the date set for his wedding. He died without recovering consciousness, leaving Maud standing among the half-made dresses of her trousseau, white-faced with fury. Mrs Broome retired to bed, as was her habit in moments of crisis, and it was left to Frances Chard to comfort Agnes as best she could.

The Broomes went into mourning. Richard was buried in the family vault, his valet departed with his ex-master's wardrobe, and Richard's dogs, which had filled the Court from morning to night with their noise, were destroyed on Maud's orders.

The heir, the Honourable Gavin Charles Broome, was campaigning in South Africa at the time of his elder brother's death. Communications with the Cape were difficult. The letter advising Gavin of Richard's death crossed with one from Gavin's commanding officer stating that Major Broome had been seriously wounded at Majuba, and was being invalided home.

Frances Chard was no gossip, but young Agnes was. Long before the new master arrived, Frances had learned that Gavin Broome had a sinister reputation, and that the servants feared rather than looked forward to his return.

At last a telegram arrived, announcing that Major Broome would be on the noon train from Lewes the following day. Three

2

months had passed since Richard's death, yet nothing was ready to welcome his successor. The servants hurriedly brushed the dust under carpets, the State Bedroom was aired, the butler sought for the key to the wine cellars.

Family and staff were drawn up on the steps of Furze Court to greet the new Lord Broome. The original family group of Mrs Broome and her two daughters had been supplemented by the recent arrival of Lady Amelia Seld and her granddaughter Isabella.

Agnes nudged her governess, and made a face at Lady Amelia's back.

'See the vultures gather,' she said. Frances suppressed a smile. It was rumoured that Lady Seld had brought her granddaughter to stay to revive the broken engagement which had once existed between Gavin Broome and Isabella. It would not be Lady Seld's fault if the Court did not soon have a new mistress. Isabella Seld was as fair as her cousin Maud was dark; she invariably wore pastel shades, in contrast to the other women of the party, who were all in mourning.

Miss Chard, standing in the background, observed Miss Seld with interest; Mrs Broome had no money of her own, and if this pale primrose of a girl, Isabella Seld, became Lady Broome, then Miss Chard's position at Furze Court might be in danger. Would such a very young girl, newly married, wish to keep a schoolgirl around? Would she not wish to

3

send Agnes away to school? In which case, Miss Chard would once more be out of a job. Miss Chard was well-educated, but she was also young and pretty, and what was more, her references were not all that they ought to be. She did not wish to lose her present position, so she watched Miss Seld, and tried to assess her. In the short time at her disposal before the carriage came into sight, Miss Chard came to the conclusion that Miss Seld was exceedingly pretty, and exceedingly nervous.

'Whatever is the matter with the man!' demanded Lady Seld. The carriage, instead of bowling along in spanking style, was being drawn along at a walking pace. The reason why was soon apparent. Amid murmurs of horror, the slight figure of a man in a stained scarlet uniform was lifted from the carriage and carried up the steps into the Court. Miss Chard drew Agnes's head down as the body of her cousin was borne past her. One side of the soldier's dark head was covered with blood, and the left arm, which was in splints, was also coloured red.

Dr Kimpton was hastily summoned from the village and the family and staff gathered around Benson, the Major's batman, to learn what had happened. Benson was a square-cut Cockney, incoherent in his distress.

'Steady, my man,' said old Lady Amelia, who seemed to have taken charge of the proceedings. Mrs Broome had given way to her palpitations, and was prostrate on a sofa. 'Take it from the beginning.'

Benson started again. His master had been badly wounded at Majuba, at the end of January. His arm had been broken, he'd had concussion and then fever. He'd not come to himself properly until he was on board ship, when he'd recovered fast . . . 'Except for his arm, which they'd told him would need attention by some surgeon or other when he got back to London. He was playing poker and cursing us all to rights and making up to the nurses—begging your pardon, ma'am— no offence! I'd been ill, too. Dysentery, and a bit of trouble with my right knee. He said to me that he wanted to go home to see his brother before he went to London to have his arm attended to. He was worried, because he hadn't had any letters from home in months. I should explain, perhaps, if you didn't know . . . I'd served him nearly two years now, come May. We'd always got on. He said to see him home, if I wasn't pressed to get back to my family. He said . . . "Come home with me; my brother will find you a place even if I don't build"—he wanted to build a house for himself, to go back to when his soldiering days were finished. I said I didn't mind if I did. He was a bit uncertain on his feet still, and his hand wasn't . . . well, I could manage the money for him, see, and I got him tucked up in a first-class compartment at Lewes when we changed trains, and then I left him to go back to my own seat, and these two men passed me, going into his compartment. I didn't think to look at them closely. Why should I? But they were big men, both of them. Bigger than me, or him. Yet he gave a good account of himself, didn't he? Even without a weapon, and with his arm in splints . . .' Benson gulped. He looked longingly at the door through which his master had been taken. 'The door of his compartment was swinging open when I got out at the Halt here. The men were gone. I reckon they must have jumped out as the train slowed up for the bend just before the station. His watch was gone, and his pocket book was on the floor, empty. There was a discharged pistol on the seat—the ball was in his arm—and he'd been beaten over the head as well. I suppose they fired the pistol, and when that didn't kill him, they used it to . . . there was blood everywhere.' Again he looked at the door. 'Is that doctor any good? Perhaps Lord Broome could send for someone from London . . .?' He looked around the Great Hall, but there was no man to be seen, except in the huddle of servants in the background. 'Two men,' he said, 'one wearing a new tweed coat, with checks on it. I didn't see their faces . . .'

'My nephew was killed just before Christmas,' said Mrs Broome in a trembling voice. 'Didn't your master know?'

Benson shook his head. He appeared

stunned.

Dr Kimpton appeared. He was an old man, and ill, due for retirement, but he had served the Broome family for many years and was a great favourite with Mrs Broome. He shook his head.

'I'm much afraid—still unconscious—you must prepare yourself for the worst.' He took Mrs Broome's hand and patted it.

'Oh, my heart!' she cried. Her maid was summoned, and she was borne off to bed. Agnes clung to her governess's hand and would not release her hold even when bidden to join her great-aunt and cousin Isabella by the fire. Miss Chard said that Agnes had had quite enough excitement for one day, and perhaps the ladies would excuse them?

'Get her back to Nurse,' snapped Maud. Of all those present, Maud appeared least affected.

As Miss Chard led Agnes away, they distinctly heard Maud say, 'So you may not have to marry him, after all, Isabella!'

*   *   *

The house was in a ferment of activity. Old Nurse was kept in the State Bedroom to which the injured man had been taken, and Miss Chard had to be very firm with a passing housemaid in order to get any tea for the schoolroom. Like Nurse, the butler was long

7

past retirement age, but the housekeeper was efficient enough and gradually a semblance of order was restored. The schoolroom was fed with news by housemaids bringing trays of food and scuttles full of coal. Miss Chard did not normally indulge in gossip, but she was as eager as Agnes to learn what was happening.

Dr Kimpton was still in attendance at supper-time, and had sent for nurses and a second opinion from Lewes. His nephew, who had only just qualified as a doctor, had joined him in the sick-room. Mrs Broome had had hysterics and her maid, Meakins, was nowhere to be found. The Blue Bedroom was to be made ready to receive Mr John Manning, an elderly relative from London; and lastly, the new heir, one Hugo Broome, was to be sent for.

'Oh, him!' said Agnes, with a twist of her shoulders. 'Well, I suppose it's a good thing that Gavin's past caring, or he'd have a fit. He hates Hugo. If you want to know what I think: I think Gavin only made up to Isabella because he couldn't bear the thought of Hugo's stepping into his shoes.'

'What is he like?' asked Miss Chard. If Hugo Broome were to inherit, then he would be her next employer.

'One of the big, fair Broomes. You know they're all either big and fair like Richard, or small and dark like Gavin and me? Only Hugo's not really like Richard. He's . . .

oh, I don't know. He creeps up behind you sometimes and makes you jump, and he never laughs at jokes. He just sort of smiles, with his hand half over his mouth. He hasn't any money of his own, so he's bound to marry Isabella, now.'

'But I didn't think Miss Seld had any money, either,' said Miss Chard.

'She hasn't. Not till Gavin dies. But Gavin's got a lot of money of his own, and before he went back to South Africa he made a Will leaving it to Isabella. So when Gavin dies, Isabella will get the money, and Hugo will get the Court, and they'll get married, and what will happen to us?'

*   *   *

Furze Court was hushed. Everyone waited. The doctor from Lewes agreed with Dr Kimpton that the case was hopeless. The arm was in a bad way, they said. They would consider amputation if their patient could stand the operation, but as it was . . .

Nurse gave up her post in the sick-room, saying it was too much for her, at her age. The two agency nurses seemed to know what they were doing, although one of them spent more of her time gossiping with the servants than on duty in the sick-room. Mr John Manning arrived from London, and so did the new heir, Mr Hugo Broome. Mr Manning spent most of

9

his time closeted with Mrs Broome, but Hugo paced the Court, his eyes into everything, as if he owned it already. Miss Chard knew that it would be sensible for her to ingratiate herself with Mr Hugo, but she could not bring herself to do so. She felt his eyes following her, as she went to and fro with Agnes; it was not a comfortable feeling. She told herself that she had no business to be forming opinions of her betters, but there it was; she did not like the man. She could not fault his appearance, which was handsome; or his manners, which were those of a gentleman. Maud certainly seemed to find her cousin everything that was charming, but Agnes . . .? Yes, there Miss Chard could fault Mr Hugo's manners, for he seemed chillingly indifferent to the fact that Agnes Broome was very upset by her cousin Gavin's condition.

Sometimes it seemed to Miss Chard as if Agnes were the only person in the whole of the Court who cared whether Gavin Broome lived or died, or grieved that he had started to refuse food and drink. Twice Agnes went down to the sick-room to see what was happening for herself. Her disobedience was discovered, of course, but luckily it was Miss Chard who found out what the child had done, and not one of the nurses, who might have been justifiably annoyed and complained to Mrs Broome.

'Well, I didn't see why I shouldn't go in to

see him,' Agnes said. 'No one else bothers, and I thought he might be lonely in there by himself, when the nurse had gone. Anyway, he can't like her much, because she stinks of dirt and gin. I'd be ashamed to be seen out with a dirty apron on like her, and finger-nails all grimy!' Miss Chard hid a smile, remembering the battles she had had in the past with Agnes on the subject of cleanliness.

'So I went in very quietly, in case he was asleep. I knew the nurse would be away for a while, because she keeps a bottle of gin in the cupboard in the attic where nobody else goes . . .'

'How did you know that?'

Agnes wriggled. 'I might have followed her one day. Just to see what she was doing up there by herself. Anyway, Dr Kimpton had told Mama that Gavin wasn't always asleep now, even though he wouldn't take food or drink. But he was asleep, and the room . . . Ugh! It stinks. Don't you think that's awful, Miss Chard? It can't make him want to get better if he's left in dirty sheets and nightshirt and not shaved, even if he is so ill. Then he woke up and I think he saw me, but I'm not sure, because he looked at me as if he didn't recognise me, and I ran for the door. And that's when I fell over and hurt myself. I'd slipped on this glass stopper which had fallen on the floor by the bed, and I picked it up and brought it away with me. I didn't really mean

11

to steal it.'

She held on to the glass stopper with both hands. It was cut-glass and looked as if it had come from a decanter. Miss Chard had noticed Agnes trying to hide it, and had demanded to know where it had come from.

'I'm not going to put it back,' said Agnes, in a voice which informed her governess that she'd better not try to take it by force, either. 'Gavin would have been very happy to give it to me, if he'd known I wanted it. He always treated me nicely, not like some people I could mention!'

'It would be stealing, if you don't have permission,' said Miss Chard. 'You must ask Mr Hugo if you may have it, after . . . when everything is settled.'

'Cousin Hugo isn't interested in old things. He pretended he was when he first came, because he thought it was expected of him, but you could see he wasn't interested when I showed him Grandpa's collection of firearms and armour. He didn't even like the ducking stool, or the pillory, so you can see he wouldn't be interested in this. Look: it's a prism. I'm going to keep it in the nursery, to make patterns on the wall for the sun to shine through.'

'You must return it, my dear. Otherwise some servant may be accused of stealing or breaking it. You wouldn't want someone else to suffer because you made a mistake, would

12

you?'

Agnes gulped. 'I don't want to go back in there again. He looks so . . . hairy, and bony and dirty. Not like him at all.' She burst into tears.

Miss Chard put her arms round the child and hugged her. 'There, now. Shall we return it together? Let us go and ask the nurse if your cousin is feeling well enough to receive visitors. If not, I will ask her to return the stopper, and no one need ever be the wiser.'

'Those nurses,' said Agnes, reluctantly following Miss Chard down the turret stairs to the Oak Gallery from which the main bedrooms led. 'They don't care what happens to him, and neither does anyone else. Mama only thinks what a worry it is having so many guests, and how she is to balance the table at dinner, and Great-aunt Amelia is always scolding Isabella for not making herself agreeable to Hugo, and Maud and Hugo spend all their time together and from the way they look at each other you can see it would be a waste of time Isabella even trying to attract Hugo's attention . . .'

It was cold in the Gallery, and both Miss Chard and Agnes pulled their shawls more closely around their shoulders. Their footsteps echoed on the wide wooden floorboards. Dingy family portraits hung on the panelled walls between the doors of the bedrooms, while opposite, between leaded windows,

13

heavy oak chests were spaced. It was dusk, and the park outside could barely be seen.

'The footmen are late bringing round the lamps,' said Miss Chard.

'I'm scared,' said Agnes.

Miss Chard wanted to say that there was nothing to be scared of, but the words died in her mouth. She knocked on the door of the State Bedroom. There was no reply. The silence in the Gallery was profound. A board creaked. Agnes jumped. Miss Chard knocked again, and the door, which could not have been properly closed, swung open. From within came a moan which raised the hairs on the back of Miss Chard's neck.

Agnes clasped her hands over her mouth and fled back along the Gallery and up the stairs to the safety of her nursery. Frances Chard raised a hand to smooth the hair at the nape of her neck, and hesitated. Should she go after Agnes? No, the child would be safe for a moment. Her old nurse was upstairs. It would only take a few minutes to restore the stopper.

She slipped into the bedroom, and looked around her. It was even darker here than it had been in the Gallery. The room was furnished with heavily carved dark oak furniture, and the four-poster bed and windows were hung with red brocade curtains. It was a sombre apartment. Beyond the bed a large mirror hung over a cavernous fireplace, reflecting in its speckled depths that part of the room which was hidden from Frances by the bed. Beyond the fireplace a door stood ajar, presumably leading into a dressing-room.

There was no one to be seen.

Frances drew in her breath. Agnes's remarks about dirt had been justified. She thought the room could not have been aired for days.

She called, 'Nurse?' No one replied.

She did not care to look at the bed closely. She was not there out of curiosity, to gawp at a dying man. She spied a clutter of medicine bottles and glasses on a table between the windows. No doubt the stopper had come from one of them.

Someone moaned on the far side of the bed. Frances' eyes went to the mirror. She glimpsed a grey shape which writhed and then subsided back on to the floor. The moans, the dusk, the seclusion, all combined to upset the governess's equilibrium. Like Agnes, she put both hands over her mouth to stifle a cry, but unlike Agnes she did not flee.

'What's all this, then?' demanded a sleepy but human voice. The tousled figure of Benson, dressed—or rather, half-dressed— appeared in the doorway of the dressing-room. Before she could flounder out an explanation of her presence, he cried out, 'Crissake! The Major!', and plunged into the gloom on the far side of the bed.

Pulling what looked like a bundle of old

clothes off the floor, he swung it towards the windows. It was one of the agency nurses, Nurse Moon by name, and she was undoubtedly the worse for drink. She staggered, rebounded off the table and sank into a sprawl on the floor. The fumes of gin and vomit were overpowering.

Frances hammered open a window, and then went to help Benson. The batman was kneeling on the floor beside something which the nurse's body had previously concealed from sight. A bolster from the bed lay partly over the face of his master. The slim body was clad in a rumpled nightshirt, badly stained. There was a discoloured bandage round the injured man's brow; the splints had been removed from his arm, and another bandage wound round his left forearm. This second bandage was not doing its duty, for it barely covered the tip of an open wound from which blood was now crawling to drip on the carpet.

'She's murdered him!'

Frances felt the sick man's pulse. 'No, he's still alive. Help me lift him back on the bed.'

'Not on those sheets,' cried Benson, beside himself with grief and rage. He pointed to the soiled bed-linen. 'That filthy, drunken crew! Christ's sake! The Major was always so particular . . . it's enough to make him ill, never mind what the doctors and the nurses have done to him between them . . . help me wash and change him, and put clean sheets on

16

the bed!'

Frances drew back. That was none of her work, as he must know.

'I'll ring the bell for a servant, who will fetch the other nurse.'

'The bell's broke, and the other nurse will have gone off to the village for the afternoon.' Benson stroked his master's forehead and tried to get some water between his lips. The invalid shuddered. His eyes opened and he began to struggle, his eyes dilated.

'It's all right, Major. The battle's over. Benson, reporting for duty, sir.' The sick man relaxed and closed his eyes. His chest rose and fell rapidly, indicating distress. He was unkempt and emaciated, but Frances did not think he looked particularly villainous; intelligent, yes, and possibly humorous, but not vicious or dissipated. His mouth, under a curved moustache, was well-shaped. Benson babbled soothing nonsense as he bathed his master's face and arm. Frances, unasked, fetched clean water and cloths from the wash-stand in the dressing-room. The sick-room was littered with the impedimenta of nursing, but nothing in it seemed clean. The water in the bowl Benson had been holding was discoloured, and the glass from which the sick man drank had previously held some yellowish liquid which had left a deposit on the bottom. There were bottles, bloodstained splints, soiled bandages and dirty crockery on trays and

17

even on the floor. If the sick man were at all conscious of his surroundings—and Frances thought she had seen the flash of intelligence in his eyes before weakness overcame him— then he must feel his neglect acutely.

'Hold him for me while I get a clean nightshirt,' Benson commanded, and Frances took the invalid into her arms without a word of protest. She was a warm-hearted girl, and it was not in her nature to refuse help to anyone who needed her, whatever he might or might not have done. Lord Broome started at the touch of a stranger's arms. She spoke to him soothingly and, feeling him shiver with cold, wrapped him in her own shawl.

'Why isn't there a fire in here?' she asked.

'Too much trouble for them lazy, thieving servants. Also they say Lord Richard never had a fire in here, so what do we want with one. I did hear one say the chimney was blocked, but it looks all right to me.'

Frances frowned. She had a fire in the schoolroom, Nurse had a fire in the day and night nurseries, there were fires in all the reception-rooms and in every one of the main bedrooms—except this.

Benson brought in a thick, coarse nightshirt, very unlike the fine cambric of the one Lord Broome wore at present. 'Mine,' he said, by way of explanation. 'I sleep next door on a cot, so that I can watch over him at night. I was just having a kip when you came, as a matter

18

of fact. I don't know what they've done with his linen.' She helped him strip Lord Broome, wash him, and reclothe him.

'A Zulu spear did that,' said Benson, seeing her look at a long, puckered scar on his master's ribs. 'Major Mercury they call him, because he's quick and deadly. Wounded twice. Decorated three times. Just luck, he says. But it was more than that.'

The invalid's eyes were half-open, but not properly focused, as if he saw everything through a mist of pain. His lips moved. Frances guessed he was asking for water. She lifted a glass that lay nearby and put it to his lips. After one sip he closed his lips and turned his head away.

'He's dying,' said Benson, 'but he won't drink that. Everything they give him has that yellow medicine in it, and he can't abide it. What I say is, if he doesn't like it, why force it on him? I've asked for gruel and tea and broth for him, but they tell me to mind my own business, and forbid me to give him anything for fear of upsetting him. Them and their theories! What do they know about what he likes? I've tried him with some of my own supper, and a jug of water and some beer and barley water that I've brought up here, on the sly. He takes that all right. But I have to do it in secret, at night, when there's just the two of us, and the nurses can't see. They said they'd get me barred from the sick-room altogether if I interfered with him in any way. That's why I couldn't shave him. They'd have noticed, see. I can feed him, on the quiet, but I can't shave him. Now, you won't tell on me, will you, Miss? I can't be doing him any harm. Why, last night he'd have had all of my supper if I hadn't thought it wrong for him to eat so much: so quickly, after having been starved like he has been.'

Frances sniffed at and then sipped the liquid in the glass. She decided that she wouldn't have wanted to drink it, either. There was a tray nearby, set with tea things for one; presumably for the nurse. The tea-cup stank of gin, and the tea was cold, but when Frances held the jug of milk to the sick man's lips, he drank it all, and seemed eager for more.

The nurse snored, arms and legs spread wide. The neck of a bottle protruded from a pocket in her dress. The vomit on the apron, added to the smell of gin which lingered around her despite the open window, explained how his lordship had come to be on the floor to Frances' satisfaction, if not to Benson's.

'The murderess!' he muttered. He had brought through some coarse sheets from the dressing-room, stripped the bed and remade it. The sheets were not big enough to cover the bed properly, and they had been slept in before, but they were far cleaner than those he took off. Frances fed the invalid the slices of bread and butter on the nurse's tray. He ate them with relish.

'You see?' said Benson. 'Knocks on the head is funny things. Likely the Major didn't know who he was or where he was at first, but I reckon he's pulling out of it. I told the doctors so, but they wouldn't listen. You can see for yourself that he'll eat and drink normally when he doesn't have to take that medicine. Up we get now, Major. On to the bed.'

The sick man had by now so far recovered as to understand what was being said to him. Obedient to Benson's suggestion, he tried to help them as they bent to lift him on to the bed. Putting his weight on his left arm, he gave a gasp of pain and fainted. Frances caught him as he crumpled against her, and cried to Benson to fetch the doctor. Blood was once more seeping down the left arm.

'Doctors! They're worse nor vets, and that's saying something!' Benson had gone pale, but he kept his head. Under his direction Frances helped him to lift Lord Broome on to the bed and cover him over. Then Benson bathed his master's forehead and told Frances to chafe the sick man's right hand.

'Just don't touch that left arm of his, Miss. They never ought to have taken the splints off . . . it wasn't ready . . . or if they had to take the splints off to get at the bullet . . . they shot him, you see, Miss. Probably thcy aimcd at his head and he put his arm up and took the ball

21

just below the elbow, just above where his arm was broken at Majuba. The doctors tried to get the bullet out, but it's lodged deep and they only made matters worse. They left it, thinking they'd kill him if they pulled him around any more, and I reckon they were right, then. The Major couldn't have stood it, what with losing so much blood . . . those two men beat him up something cruel, and I never noticed them when they passed me . . . I told the police I didn't think I'd know them again . . . There, now. He's coming round again. Now where can I get him some more food and drink without it being covered with that yellow poison?'

'The tea tray may still be in the schoolroom. Miss Agnes wasn't hungry and I never eat at tea-time. Do you know where the schoolroom is?'

The Court was built in the form of a hollow square around the cloisters of the abbey which had once stood on the site. The Great Hall occupied the north side of the Court, and the south side was occupied by the Oak Gallery and the principal bedrooms. The reception-rooms and the tower which contained the apartments occupied by Mrs Broome occupied the west side of the Court, and on the east side were the quarters for the staff, kitchens, servants' hall, and so on. On the floor above the domestic offices were the schoolroom, nurseries, and sleeping quarters of the staff. This floor could be reached by turret staircases leading from the main floor at the end of the Oak Gallery, and also from beside the servants' hall. Thus, the schoolroom lay one floor above and at right angles to the principal bedroom. Benson nodded, and withdrew.

It was the hour between tea and the time to dress for dinner, when the family would be occupied in the Great Hall or the gun-room. This side of the Court was deserted. In theory Frances ought to have sent Benson for servants to fetch food from the kitchen, but she was a practical person, and knew it would take a good half-hour to obtain any food through the usual channels; and then there was always the point that his lordship would refuse it if adulterated with the yellow powder.

The invalid seemed uneasy. He turned his head from side to side; perhaps he was aware that Benson had left him. Frances spoke to him reassuringly, and he managed to locate her face and fix his eyes on her. He reminded her of Agnes, who also had clear, light-grey eyes. The left side of his head had been badly bruised, but the stains were fading.

She found she was still holding his right hand. She averted her eyes from his left arm. The bandage round his forearm had slipped, or been badly tied. It was too tight, and yet too low to cover the wound. The flesh beneath was no sight for a weak stomach. The scar of the earlier wound was puckered and barely healed. The open wound above showed where the doctors had probed for the buried bullet. The left thumb and forefinger seemed, even to her untrained eye, to be limp and possibly smaller than they ought to have been.

She told herself that she could—no, ought not to interfere with the dressing on his arm, however much it needed attention. She listened for the footsteps of a passing servant. She wished she had insisted that Benson go for the doctor straightaway.

There was a sharp pair of scissors and fresh bandages on the bedside table, beside a pile of books. She read the titles: a worn Bible, Ruskin, St Simon, Gibbons' *Decline and Fall* . . . these would be the property of Gavin, not Richard Broome. The previous Lord Broome had held all books in contempt.

Blood was welling from the injured arm. She leaned over to touch the sick man's left hand. Lord Broome stiffened, but his eyes did not leave her face. She spoke to him, explaining that she was going to change his dressings, that it would hurt, but only for a moment, and that he would feel better afterwards. He sighed as she cut through the discoloured bandages and gently bathed the wound beneath. She talked to him while she worked, and to her surprise he cooperated. The bandage round his head was badly stained, but the wounds beneath were almost healed. His hair was thick and dark without any grey in it. Richard had been thirty-seven when he died, so this man must

24

be something less, though he looked about the same age. He smiled at her as she laid him back on the pillows, and she thought his lips were trying to form the words 'Thank you'.

'Oh, yes,' she said. 'I can see you are used to getting your own way; but you will allow me to tell you that you are far too thin and that I prefer my men clean-shaven.'

The invalid smiled again, having understood her tone, but not the sense of what she said.

When Benson returned with a laden tea-tray, he commended Frances for her work.

'That's all very well,' said Frances, feeding Lord Broome more milk and bread and butter, 'but we've interfered with the nurses' routine with a vengeance. What are they going to say when they see what we've done?'

'This one won't say nothing,' said Benson. He seized Nurse Moon under the shoulders and dragged her towards the door. 'It's a piece of luck that you came in today, for you can help me get rid of the nurses, and have his medicine changed. They wouldn't listen to me when I complained about them, but they'll listen to you.'

'I doubt it. I must go as soon as I have fed him this. It is not my job to . . .'

'Nor is it mine, Miss. What if he did nurse me when I was down to skin and bone with dysentery, and could only hobble about with a stick? And again when I was ill on the ship coming home, and he could barely hold

25

himself upright? I've paid him back, haven't I? He asked me to see him safely home, and make sure the doctors didn't take his arm off on the way, and I've done that. I've no need to hang around now, when I've a family in London that I've not seen for a couple of years.' He got the door propped open, and went back for the nurse. 'Drat that door. The key's missing and it won't stay open. It won't stay shut when you want it to, neither. And drat this nasty, draughty house, and drat the servants who won't lift a finger for him, and drat his family who don't give a damn . . . sorry, Miss . . . don't give a hang for what becomes of him. "Poor Gavin!" they say, coming in here without so much as asking if it's convenient, night or day. "Poor Gavin!" they say, but they really mean, "How inconvenient it is that he's taking so long to die!" '

Frances shook her head at him. 'You must not talk like that, you know.'

'Why not? It's the truth. You are the first person to give him a kind word. You speak soft and gentle and he likes that. I heard you singing the other evening . . . it was you, wasn't it? Up in the schoolroom? I had the window open, airing the room, and he heard it, too. He lifted his head and opened his eyes and although he didn't know me, it was the first time he'd shown any real sign that he was coming out of it. I remember it well, because you were singing a song he always used to hum when we was on the march. Lillibullero. I reckon it reminded him, hearing you sing that song.'

'Flattery will get you nowhere.' Frances stood up and smoothed her dress. 'I must go. Miss Agnes will be needing me.'

'You will come again? You will speak to Mrs Broome about getting the nurses out of the place? I can manage him better by myself.'

'I . . . no, he is not my responsibility. Besides, you cannot possibly manage by yourself.'

'She tried to kill him, you know.'

'She was drunk.'

'And where did she get her gin from?'

'I have heard that she kept a bottle hidden in one of the cupboards upstairs.'

'One bottle wouldn't last her more nor a day. And money. She had plenty of it. Where did that come from?'

The questions hung in the air, unanswered. A nurse's wages were small. One of the few rules on which Mrs Broome insisted was that none of the servants should drink in her house. Frances' uneasiness grew. She pulled the glass stopper out of her pocket and held it out to Benson. 'I must go. I only came to return this.'

'It's not ours.'

'Not . . .? But . . . Well, never mind. I must go now.'

'Be off, then!' cried Benson, reddening with anger. 'No one in this house will blame you for

27

refusing to be a good Samaritan, will they? I hope you have nightmares of him lying here, suffering, when you go to bed tonight . . .'

'What is all this?' enquired a languid voice. Hugo Broome stood in the doorway, and behind him was Mr Manning. Neither of them looked pleased by what they saw. Frances started, and knocked a book off the bedside table. As it fell to the floor, a stiff, folded sheet of paper fell out and fluttered along the carpet. Hugo Broome picked it up, but not before they had all seen what was written on the outside. It was a Last Will and Testament.

'Why . . .! This is . . .' Hugo scanned the Will—it was short—and passed it to his uncle, while his normally placid expression altered to fierce joy, before being returned to normal. 'This Will,' he said to his uncle, 'cancels the one Gavin made earlier. It leaves everything to Maud!'

Frances looked at the sick man, fearful that he might have been distressed by hearing raised voices, but he was asleep. Or, at least, his eyes were fast shut. As she looked, his eyelids quivered. She had seen children's eyelids quiver like that when they were pretending to be asleep and knew they were being watched.

Mr John Manning said, 'It looks all right, but . . . we must consider! Hugo, this must be kept quiet until it is looked into.'

Benson was scratching his head. 'That's

not the Major's, is it?' He looked genuinely puzzled. 'What the 'ell is going on?'

'What, indeed!' said Mr Manning, taking charge of the situation. 'What exactly are you doing here, with that woman at your feet? And what is the meaning of your presence, Miss Chard?'

CHAPTER TWO

It was not often that Frances was required by Mrs Broome at the dinner table, but that night there were several guests, so Frances was required to balance the numbers. The fading hand of decay might be at work elsewhere at Furze Court, but by candlelight the dining-room still looked beautiful. Family portraits hung the walls. Over the mantelpiece was a full-length portrait of Richard Broome with two of his dogs at his feet; his brother smiled at him from the background.

Frances, seated between the vicar and Dr Kimpton's nephew, was furthest from the warmth of the fire, but in a good position to inspect the portrait.

The newly qualified doctor, Theo Green, followed the direction of her eyes, and wondered aloud which artist Hugo Broome would choose to paint him when he succeeded to the title. 'Although I expect Maud will want a say in the matter. It's a pity they won't have any money, but there's no denying they'll make a handsome couple.'

Theo was a shrewd young man with a brusque manner. His training had been sound, but he had yet to learn how to please influential hypochondriacs like Mrs Broome. He had met Frances several times before, when he had been called in to treat minor ailments amongst the staff. She liked him well enough, and had once or twice speculated on the warmth of his regard for her.

She smiled at him. 'Have I been neglecting you? Forgive me. I am quite in disgrace, you know, for interfering in the sick-room.'

'Nonsense,' said Theo, attacking his food with the energetic movements characteristic of him. 'Something had to be done. The way the sick-room was being run was a scandal. If my uncle had not been so unwell lately . . .' he looked across the table to where Dr Kimpton was trying to smother a cough. 'He did mention it to Mrs Broome, you know, but it is so difficult to get trained staff to come out here, that nothing was done. Nurse Moon has departed, I assume?'

'Oh, yes. Mr Hugo saw to that. She was packed off back to Lewes on the next train. I don't know how they are going to manage without her; for all that Benson wants to nurse his master on his own, he is not able to watch around the clock. The other agency nurse

30

seems to spend more of her time in the village or the servants' hall than in the sick-room.'

'My uncle asked me to bring the midwife from the village to sit with him tonight, so that Benson could get some rest. You have no experience of nursing, yourself?'

Frances shook her head. She was feeling subdued. The last thing she wanted was to have attention drawn to herself—or her references. For the umpteenth time she resolved to keep herself to herself, to act with decorum at all times, and never ever to become embroiled in the affairs of the family again. Nevertheless, she could not help wondering about the new Will which Hugo had picked up and which Mr Manning had taken into safe keeping. If she had understood the matter correctly, this new Will left everything to Maud. It was evident from the doctor's remarks that he knew nothing of this. Did Maud know?

Frances looked down the table, to where Maud's head was bent close to Hugo's. Maud was all vivacity this evening. She sparkled, she bent her long white neck coquettishly, she flashed her fan and showed her sharp white teeth, and all this display was for Hugo. There was no doubt that Maud was as much taken with Hugo as he was with her.

Were his attentions serious? Would she indeed be the next mistress of the Court? Frances had had plenty of time to form an opinion of Maud's character, and to observe the selfishness which was Miss Broome's chief characteristic. Maud treated Agnes as if she were of rather less importance than a dog. Frances would have no future at the Court if Maud became Lady Broome.

Did Isabella know that she had been disinherited? It did not look as if she did. She sat between her uncle, Mr Manning, and Dr Kimpton, and she smiled dreamily to herself.

The vicar cleared his throat. It was time for Frances to turn her attention to him.

'I hear the new Lord Broome has lost the will to live,' he said. He was a heavy-set man, humourless but conscientious. 'A distaste for food, the doctors say. Ah, well. No doubt his crimes weigh heavily upon him. Dr Kimpton tells me he has occasional intervals of consciousness. We must see what we can do. We will wrestle with his soul and, God willing, bring him to repentance before he goes to meet his Maker.'

'What crimes?' said Frances. 'Forgery? Rape? Murder?'

The vicar turned his eyes on her and frowned. 'It is not seemly to speak of such matters with levity.'

'No. I am sorry.'

'A pity that the great-uncle's fortune was left to Gavin, and not to Richard, or we might have got a new organ in the church. Gavin did not have his brother's frank, open temperament. Even before the affair of the

32

lodgekeeper's wife . . . poor woman! . . .' He shook his head, and sighed. 'After that, of course, he was ostracised. If it had not been for his rank, and the esteem in which his brother was held, I really believe Gavin might have had to stand his trial. I am amazed— no, astounded—that he has had the nerve to return here, but at least it will give me an opportunity of urging the value of repentance on him.' He helped himself to some more turbot.

As soon as Frances was able to turn back to Theo, she asked him to tell her what it was that Lord Broome had done to deserve the vicar's disapproval.

'Don't you believe it,' said Theo shortly. 'A pack of lies. I wasn't here at the time—I was in my final year up at Bartholomew's in London—but I heard about it. I thought it would all have been forgotten by now. Perhaps it would, if Gavin hadn't had to step into his brother's shoes. Believe me, Gavin's not like that. He never courted popularity, of course. He would never put up with shoddy service, and the servants didn't like him because he was always on at Richard to retrench. Richard had no money of his own, but you wouldn't have thought so, from the way he lived. Take it from me, Gavin's all right. He was always kind to me. Not just carelessly kind like Richard, but putting himself out to help. Like teaching me how to tie a fly for trout-fishing,

33

and advising me on buying my first hunter. And he taught me to box a bit, too, for I was undersized and clumsy as a schoolboy.'

'He hardly looks strong enough.'

'His looks are deceptive. He's tough, and quick-witted. No one here had the brains to appreciate him. They all thought Richard was marvellous because he was big and handsome and had never read a book in his life. Gavin was bookish, and invested his money cleverly; they say he doubled the fortune he inherited. And yet he had such a droll way of expressing himself . . . Sorry, I'm getting maudlin.' He thumped the table. 'I wish I knew what was wrong with him. It's not like him to give up like this. Why is he starving himself to death? Surely not because of what happened last summer?'

'He's not eating or drinking what the nurses provide because he doesn't like the yellow powder you doctors have ordered for him.'

'What yellow powder? To be put on his food? There is a meat extract which my uncle recommended, but nothing else that I can think of.'

'Something with a burning taste. Acid. It is yellowish in colour and quite horrible. I don't blame him for refusing anything adulterated with that stuff.'

The doctor looked disquieted, but had to suspend his conversation, for Mrs Broome had given the signal for the ladies to rise from the table. Theo waited for the port to come his way, and thought that, if his uncle did not object, he would like to pay a visit to the sick-room later that night.

*   *   *

Mrs Moon, dismissed from her post at Furze Court, was followed home to Lewes. She did not suspect anything. She was acquainted with the man who followed her, but she was too bound up in her own miseries to notice that he boarded the compartment next to hers at Furze Halt, or that soft but heavy footstep followed her through the streets to the cottage in which she lived.

The man in the checked overcoat paused when he reached her door, and glanced up and down the street. Then he knocked with the head of his hickory stick, and was let in.

'You muffed it,' he said.

'Couldn't help it. That governess came in, and knocked me out.'

'It was the drink that knocked you out, not her. We don't like people making a muff of things.'

'You should have seen I got another chance, if you've got such a pull at the Court.'

'You had plenty of chances.'

'I did everything you said. I put that yellow stuff on everything he had to eat and drink, and I saw that no one else fed him or went too

35

close to him, except for Benson, and he was too stupid to see what was going on. You only had to wait, and he'd have starved himself to death.'

'Where's the bottle of the yellow stuff?'

She handed it over. 'Now for me money,' she said. 'Payment on delivery, you said.'

'This is it,' said the man, and swung his stick at her head. She cried out, but only once. The thud of the stick on a woman's body was not an uncommon sound in that poor area of the town. Presently the man stopped. He searched her cottage in case she had written anything down, and then left. No one saw him go, except for a pale child in a doorway, who admired his checked overcoat.

*   *   *

Even in 1881 it was commonly believed that women were impractical, fanciful creatures who filled their heads with romantic nonsense. Men, having had the advantage of a better education, and having been endowed with a superior brain, were supposed to be practical, and impatient of fantasy. It is therefore remarkable that while Miss Chard, who was occasionally guilty of reading romances, dismissed Benson's talk of murder and poison as nonsense, the level-headed London-trained doctor did not.

Dr Kimpton was still coughing by the time

36

the port had gone round twice; when Theo suggested that he should save his uncle trouble by making the routine visit to the sick-room on his behalf, the offer was gratefully accepted.

So Theo paid his visit, and listened to everything that Benson had to say, and while laughing at himself for doing so, looked carefully around the sick-room for any sign of the yellow powder of which Benson and Miss Chard had complained. He found none. Frances' interference might have raised eyebrows in the servants' hall, but it had been effective in drawing the attention of Mr Manning and Hugo to the state of neglect which reigned in the sick-room. Gone were the dirty crocks, sheets and dressings. The room had been swept and dusted, a fire had been lighted in the grate, and although the sick man slept lightly, he had little or no fever. Mrs Peach, the midwife from the village, had arrived, and was all set to take the night watch. Theo came to the conclusion that Benson was over-tired, and jealous of the nurses. That his wild accusations of murder and poison were, in short, due to fatigue.

Only, as he went out of the sick-room he thought he heard footsteps scurrying away. Had someone been listening outside the door? That was something else which Benson had complained about. The Gallery was badly lit, but empty. Theo stepped to the windows. A few flakes of snow twisted past the panes. A door closed softly at the end of the Gallery, and he turned sharply, wanting to see who might be spying on him. There was no one there.

Spying on him? What nonsense! Servants . . . natural curiosity . . . no trace of any yellow powder . . . all in the imagination!

The family always gathered in the music-room after dinner. This was a long, narrow apartment occupying the whole of the west side of the Court, which had oriel windows overlooking the park on one side, and the cloisters within. Frances was often summoned to sit with the family in the evenings because, being a proficient musician, she could accompany Maud on the piano if that lady wished to sing, or soothe Mrs Broome's nerves by playing some of the melodies of her youth to her. No one ever suggested that Frances might entertain the company in her own right, although she had a prettier voice than Maud.

Lady Amelia sat close to the fireplace, playing patience. Mrs Broome complained gently to Dr Kimpton about her nervous spasms, while managing to ignore his appalling cough. Mr Manning and Hugo had their heads close together by the bureau, although now and then Hugo turned his head to watch Maud, who was walking up and down the room with Isabella. The vicar voiced the question in everyone's mind when Theo appeared.

'How is he?'

'Asleep.'

There was an almost audible sigh of disappointment from everyone. Theo made his way to where Miss Chard was sitting over some tapestry work. He thought she looked far more of a lady than Maud, who was over-dressed and whose manners were not pleasing; or Isabella, who had nothing but a certain youthful prettiness to commend her. There was a reddish tinge to the heavy coils of Miss Chard's hair which offset her clear skin and grey eyes to perfection ... or so the doctor thought. Her movements had a grace which Maud could only imitate. She had a warmth of personality which aroused positive feelings of admiration or dislike wherever she went. Theo was beginning to think that although her youth, beauty and forcefulness were a handicap to her as a governess, such qualities might well grace the wife of an ambitious young doctor. He sat down beside her.

'Asleep?' she repeated. 'Not shamming?'

'No, really asleep. He ate a custard tonight, Benson says. There's a loyal fellow for you. He's worn himself out, looking after his master. But if he goes around telling everyone that his master is in imminent danger of being murdered in his bed, he'll get into trouble. I did think of ordering him out of the sick-room, till he's had a good rest.'

'No, no. That would be too cruel. You mustn't separate them now. Besides, you could

39

see how Benson came to think such a thing. I saw him pull Nurse Moon off Lord Broome with my own eyes. She was lying on top of him, in a drunken stupor. There was a bolster over Lord Broome's face. I assume that she had been trying to make some adjustments to the bedclothes, but, being drunk, had fallen, and in falling had grabbed at him and pulled him off the bed with her. It is quite true that the accident could have been fatal. I think Benson has every right to be angry. But to talk of murder . . . no. Except . . .'

She suspended her needle. It was one of the polite fictions of life at the Court that Mrs Broome was embroidering a new set of covers for the chairs in the music-room, but in fact the work was carried out by whoever happened to be governess at the time.

'You are thinking of Benson's talk of mysterious midnight visitors? Of missing keys, and doors that open and shut by themselves?'

'Good gracious, no. There's nothing wrong in members of his family calling into the sick-room to see how he does, is there? And as for the door; well, it is true that it doesn't shut properly, but there is nothing mysterious about a defective lock.'

'Then why are you worried? You have been worried all evening, haven't you?'

'I hardly know why. Each incident can be explained away, except . . .'

'You are thinking of the yellow powder.

I found no trace of it. I can assure you that my uncle has never ordered any such thing, and neither did the doctor from Lewes. I was present at their consultation, although naturally I was not allowed to open my mouth.'

'Yet I saw it. I tasted it. It did exist. Have you asked the servants about it? If food is sent away untouched from the schoolroom, it is usually eaten by whichever of the footmen collects the tray. If you ask in the kitchens, you may be able to find someone who has tasted and rejected the dishes sent up to your patient.'

'He is not my patient. He is my uncle's. And I can't go around upsetting the servants asking that sort of question. Nurse Moon must have had some pet preparation of her own, which she used on her own initiative. Now that she is gone, and if Gavin really has started to eat again, we should see a marked improvement in his condition. In fact, if it were not for his arm, I would be inclined to quarrel with my uncle's diagnosis. I think Gavin might well pull through.'

'Oh, I am so glad.' She spoke on impulse, as always.

'Why? What is he to you?' Could Theo be jealous?

She bent her head over her work, blushing. 'Nothing,' she said, in a strained tone. 'Only, he seems always to have treated Agnes kindly, and I think my job here might be more secure

41

if he lived, than if his cousin inherited.'

The tea tray was brought in, and Frances had to leave Theo in order to pour out for Mrs Broome. A governess's time was not her own. But as she passed cups and made polite responses to whatever remarks were addressed to her, she longed for the evening to be over, so that she might be alone. Her adventure in the sick-room had disturbed her for more reasons than one; she had good reason to fear scrutiny of her private life by her employers and knew she had drawn unwelcome attention to herself by stepping out of her sphere of activity in the schoolroom. That alone would have been enough to upset her, but there was more, far more than that for her to think about.

She was aware that there are some men— and women, too—who exercise a fascination for the opposite sex independent of good looks or even of good character. She herself had this gift of attraction, and had watched with mingled pleasure and alarm while certain men of her acquaintance had made fools of themselves over her. When she had in her turn made a fool of herself over a man, she had known that she was only following a path trodden by other women before her. Walter Donne had been Frances' physical opposite; tall, dark, and swarthy of complexion. She had felt his attraction from the moment they met, but had withstood his wooing for many months because she could not believe that he was serious in his intentions towards her. The affair had ended disastrously for her. Walter had failed her in every way.

Dismissed her place at Mrs Palfrey's without a reference, under threat of prosecution for a theft of which she was innocent, she had returned to the school which her aunt ran just outside Bath, to work there as a teacher until she obtained the post at Furze Court. Frances' father had been the younger son of a well-known Somersetshire family, but he had been cast off by his family for marrying the gentle girl who died in giving birth to Frances. Colonel Chard had been killed in India five years later, and his only child left penniless. She had been brought up by her mother's sister, a hard woman, who thought to keep Frances on as unpaid teacher in her school. When Frances was eighteen she left her aunt to seek her first position as a governess, and she had only been back to Bath at rare intervals since.

When asked for references by Mrs Broome, Miss Chard had given her aunt's name, and had also referred to the lady for whom she had worked before she went to Mrs Palfrey's. Frances had explained the time lapse between the date of leaving that post and the date of her application to Mrs Broome by saying that she had subsequently been employed at her aunt's. It had been Frances' aim to make herself indispensable at the Court before her secret was discovered. She had little doubt that it would be, eventually. Some day someone who had known her in Gloucestershire would meet someone who knew the Broome family, and the story would come out. She had hoped that sometime she would have courage enough to confess everything to Mrs Broome, but she had not yet done so.

She had, she thought, been discretion itself until chance had thrown her in the way of Lord Broome. He reminded her very strongly of Walter. It was not that the men were so very alike except in colouring, but she had recognised in Lord Broome that same fascination for women which had been her own undoing where Walter had been concerned, She had not really been surprised to hear Lord Broome's name connected with that of a woman. The man had charm, and if he chose to smile in a certain way at a woman, then that woman had better look out for herself.

Frances longed to be released from the company, but when the time came for her to depart, her footsteps dragged. She was tired and discouraged and oppressed by the feeling that she was being talked about by the family now that she had left them. She was almost at the foot of the stairs when the door of the State Bedroom opened, and Benson called her back.

'Miss Chard. I was listening for you. Do you happen to know where the key to the door might be?'

'The housekeeper would know, I suppose.'

'I asked her, and she said there should be a bunch of keys hanging up in her room, but it isn't there, and she doesn't know where it's got to. The catch on this door doesn't hold properly, and what with people wandering in and out of these rooms in the middle of the night, I want to lock this door to give us both a good night's rest.'

'Have you tried the dressing-room door? There may be a key in the lock there which would fit.'

'I knew you'd think of something.' He beckoned to her. 'Come and see the Major. Sleeping like a baby with half my supper inside him, as well as some broth and an egg custard which they sent up for him earlier. They can't find his yellow powder anywhere, and all I can say is, I hope that Nurse Moon took it with her, because he can do without it.' He had donned a collar and jacket, but was still without shoes. He disappeared into the sick-room, still talking, and Frances followed him, knowing that she was foolish to expose herself once more to the sight of a man who reminded her so much of Walter, and yet unable to resist doing so.

The room had been cleaned, and was now warm. An oil lamp threw shadows across the

45

bed, and these shadows tussled with the ones thrown by the fire in the grate.

'You have done well, Benson,' said Frances, as he held back the bedcurtains so that she could see the sick man. Lord Broome stirred. He opened his eyes and looked up at her, frowning either with pain or the effort to remember who she might be. She thought: He is not at all like Walter . . . how could I have thought that he was? Her hand went out, as if of its own volition, to push the hair back from his brow.

She said, 'You are not going to die.'

He moved his head so that her hand lay along his cheek. She withdrew her hand and put it over her heart. She felt she must leave the room at once, before it was too late.

'The Major always did sleep lightly,' said Benson, nudging her arm with a glass containing a dose of medicine. 'He knows me now. Can't say my name properly yet, but he knows I'm here to help him and not to harm him. He goes by voices since he was hit on the head. Maybe his sight's not clear yet. I've known that happen. He knows my voice, and he knows yours. He didn't like the nurses, either of them. Nor the older doctors. He thinks the young doctor's all right, but he's hardly ever here. Now if you'll just give the Major this sleeping draught which the young doctor left for him . . .? He'll take food and drink from me, but he won't take any

46

medicine.'

Frances drew back. 'No. I don't want to . . .'

'You must. He fell on his bad arm, see? He can't seem to sleep for long without it troubling him. That young doctor seems to know more about such things than his uncle, and I could see he was worried about his arm, same as I am. It's only laudanum, Miss.'

'Mrs Peach . . . get her to do it.'

'She's asleep on my bed next door. I'm to rouse her at twelve, when she'll sit with him until morning. The young doctor said I was to get a good night's rest for once and I'll admit I could drop off right now, but I daren't leave him like this, with his arm hurting and that dratted door unlocked so that anybody could walk in and murder him.'

As if to lend weight to his argument, at that very moment voices were to be heard approaching the bedroom door. Frances was alarmed. She had no wish to be found in the sick-room twice in one day. Telling Benson that she would see if there were a key in the dressing-room door, she went through the communicating door, leaving it ajar behind her. The dressing-room was small. On a cot bed Mrs Peach, the midwife, slept. Large wooden cupboards lined the walls. There was a marble-topped washstand, and a hip bath. A full-length pier glass hung on a mahogany stand. This glass was so placed—presumably by Benson—that anyone lying on the bed

47

would have a view through the doorway into the sick-room beyond. A night-light burned on the washstand.

Frances had not left the sick-room a moment too early, for as she bent over the lock of the door which led out of the dressing-room back on to the Gallery, she heard Lady Amelia telling Benson that he might wait outside the sick-room. The door from the dressing-room on to the Gallery was locked, and there was no key in sight. She could not escape that way. What was she to do? It would be embarrassing to be found there, as if she were in hiding. She put up a hand to smooth her back hair. She decided to wait in the dressing-room until Lady Amelia had gone. Then she heard the old lady say, 'Come here, Isabella.' So Miss Seld was there, as well? Frances bit her lip. It was most unfortunate that she had left the door between dressing-room and sick-room ajar. She had no wish to eavesdrop, but she was going to be able to hear every word spoken next door. Ought she not to make her presence known?

'I'd prefer to wait outside, if you are going to pray over him.' That was Isabella's voice, and she sounded sullen.

'I want you to look at him. There! Doesn't the sight of him, lying there so thin and worn, move you at all? Remember what he meant to you, only a few months ago? Remember that he has left you all his money! If you cannot

48

love him, at least you can show your gratitude by helping to look after him now he is dying. His aunt is too weakly, Maud too interested in her own concerns to nurse him; but you . . . you could, couldn't you?'

'I remember only too well what he was to me. He took advantage of me, because I was young and knew no better, while all the time he was leading a double life with that whore!'

'Servants' tattle. He denied it, and I believed him. And so ought you. If you had only stood by him, my girl, no one would have believed there was anything in the story. Breaking off your engagement like that was the most damaging thing you could have done to him. It confirmed everyone's suspicions . . .'

'The woman was pregnant, remember?'

Someone sighed. There was a swirl of silk, and the door on to the Gallery banged. A moment of silence, and then the other woman also swept out, closing the door more gently as she went.

Frances found herself standing at Lord Broome's bedside without knowing how she got there. His eyes were open, his head was turned to the door, and there was an expression of puzzlement and pain on his face. It seemed that he had heard and understood enough of what had been said to disturb him.

'Oh, hush!' said Frances. It was an absurd thing to say, for he had not spoken. She took his sound hand in hers and began to stroke it, trying to think of words which might comfort him. 'You must not let her upset you. There are other girls, with warmer hearts, who would stand by you in a time of trouble. I don't know what it was that you did, but I'm sure it can't have been anything very terrible.'

She slipped her arm under his shoulders and raised him so that his head rested in the angle between her neck and shoulder. She was very conscious of her own strength, and of his weakness. She willed him to rest and to sleep. He was very tense. Remembering that Benson had said the sick man had enjoyed hearing her sing, she began to hum a lullaby. He began to relax against her. She set the sleeping draught to his lips. He refused it. She told him to behave himself. He drank it. She was pleased with him, and told him so. His eyes closed, and he breathed lightly but easily. Her shawl was still around his shoulders. She tucked it round him more closely and laid him back on the pillows; and then, absent-mindedly, almost in passing, as if she were settling a sick child down for the night, she kissed his forehead.

Only, he had not been quite asleep. His eyelids flickered. He smiled. Then turned his head slightly away from her, and fell asleep.

She put her hands over her hot cheeks. Had she really kissed him, a grown man? Why? Because he had reminded her of Walter? No, because he was not really like Walter. He was more like Agnes, and that might have been

50

why . . .

A movement at her side increased her embarrassment. Benson had observed what she had done. 'I'll not blab, Miss. It was like a blessing. I only hope that when my time comes, someone will do the same for me. I shouldn't wonder if it didn't do him more good than a dozen sleeping draughts. And he never did it, Miss. You can take my word for that.'

'You were listening at the door? Yes, of course. You would.'

'I wanted to be sure they didn't harm him.'

'But what was it that he did?'

'What was it that he didn't do, you mean? Murder, Miss. And if you haven't found the key for the door, I'll set a chair under the knob when you've gone, to keep us safe for the night.'

*   *   *

Murder! The word echoed in Frances' dreams, and kept time with her footsteps as she walked across the park to church next morning. Mur . . . der . . . Mur . . . der . . .

Snow clouds pressed low on the trees, but the wind had dropped. Only the occasional snowflake fell slowly to the earth. Attendance at church was obligatory for everyone at Furze Court. Most of the family had gone in the carriage, driving the winding mile through the park, past the lodge gates and out on to

51

the road which led through the village to the church. Agnes and Miss Seld had chosen to walk through the shrubbery, across the rickety wooden footbridge over the sullen river, and then to the door in the wall of the park, which led into the churchyard. Agnes had something on her mind, and chose not to reply when Frances spoke to her. Frances felt that this was just as well, for she had slept badly, hearing the word 'murder' in her dreams.

At first Isabella was equally silent, but on the return journey she slipped her arm through that of the governess, and begged the favour of a word with her. Agnes had run on ahead. Frances said that she ought to keep her charge in sight, especially crossing the bridge, which looked most unsafe to her.

'Yes, indeed,' said Isabella, and shivered. Once across the bridge, however, Isabella was not to be put off. She began by saying that she had seen Frances reflected in the pier-glass in the dressing-room, the night before.

Frances started, and would have given an explanation of her presence there, but Isabella was not interested in other people's concerns—only in her own.

'You were not at the Court last year, Miss Chard. I do wish you had been. I can see that you are the sort of person who can understand and sympathise. My trouble is that I have no one, absolutely no one, to talk to. Well, Gran is marvellous for her age, of course, but she can't really remember what it is like to be young and pretty. And Maud is so . . .' She did not specify exactly what she thought of Maud, but Frances nodded. 'There you are—I was sure you would understand and be able to advise me. It's about Gavin . . . Lord Broome . . . of course. I was so young, only seventeen, and everyone urged me to take him, and of course he had a lot of money and was very charming and although he hadn't got a house of his own, he had plans to build one; it was very flattering that he should pay court to me when he must have known that he could have had almost anyone; Maud has been after him for years, I know, and Susan Armstrong, and . . . well, lots of girls. And I did think it would be nice to be married and rent a house in Town for the Season and he never said or did anything to indicate that underneath . . . in fact, at first I couldn't believe it, but Maud said . . . and then, of course, it all came out at the inquest and I couldn't marry him after that, could I?'

'I'm afraid I know nothing about it.'

'He'd been carrying on with the wife of the lodge-keeper here. His name is Jervis. You must have seen him around. A big, dark man. He was very cut up about it, because it had been going on under his nose for months, and he only found out when she got pregnant. There was a row and he turned her out of the house. She came straight up to the Court and

53

was with Gavin—quite openly—for hours. I remember that because we had been going to go riding together and he put me off. Then when she came out of the gun-room, after seeing Gavin, she told the butler that she was going to live in Lewes and be a lady, and so, of course, they all guessed what had been going on, although nobody told me about it for ages. Only she didn't stay in Lewes. Perhaps if she had, if it had only been a passing thing, and someone had told me later on, after we were married, I could have forgiven him, although I could never have understood it, for she was quite impossible, you know. Her father was a gypsy.'

'You mean you could have forgiven him for a passing infatuation?'

'Y-yes. Although I must say that I was beginning to have doubts about him even before Lilien died. Lilien was her name. You see, Gavin would say something and I could never be sure whether he was laughing at me or not, and he was forever going up to London on what he called business, but as I told him, if he really was in love with me, he wouldn't always be wanting to leave me here by myself with no one to talk to.'

'What did he say to that?' asked Miss Chard, who had formed the uncharitable opinion that Isabella was one of the silliest creatures she had ever come across. She was not at all surprised that an intelligent, well-read man

54

like Gavin Broome had been amusing himself with another woman on the side.

'Oh, he tried to talk to me about politics, and investments and Uncle Manning's charities, and all that sort of boring thing. It makes me shudder,' continued Miss Seld, unconscious of the disapproval she had aroused, 'to think how nearly I married him. There was even talk of my going back to South Africa with him when his leave was up. Then Lilien gave him away. She came back to meet him in the park by the footbridge. Gavin said she slipped and fell into the river and drowned accidentally, but there was a bruise on her forehead as big as a pigeon's egg, and, of course, everyone knew that Jervis wasn't the father of the child she was carrying. The verdict at the inquest was misadventure, but afterwards, when they buried her, Lilien's father swore that he'd be revenged on the House of Broome. I didn't go to the funeral, of course, but I was told about it. So I wrote Gavin a note and said that I thought I was too young to commit myself in marriage just yet. And he came to see me, and tried to make me change my mind, and Gran said . . . and I cried and cried, but I couldn't! I just couldn't!'

'He denied it?'

'Oh, yes, of course. He would, wouldn't he? But he looked so red and so . . . as if he knew all about it really. I pretended to believe him, because I can't bear people shouting at me, but he could see I didn't really believe him. He went all stiff and stem and said he thought I was probably right about our not marrying straight away. He said he would go up to London on some business matter or other the next day, so that I needn't think of cutting short my visit to the Court on his account. And that was the last I saw of him.'

'I understand,' said Frances.

'I don't think you do,' said Isabella, laughing to distract attention from an embarrassing blush. 'It's not about that I wanted to speak to you. Or only indirectly. You see, the thing is—ought I to accept Gavin's money, seeing that it comes from a tainted source? He made a Will just before he went away, leaving everything to me apart from a small legacy to Benson and, of course, something in trust for Richard. I quite expected him to change his Will after I broke off our engagement, but he didn't. Gran thought that he had left the Will as it was, hoping that I might forget about Lilien while he was away, and that we might make up the match again on his return. We don't have any money of our own, you see, and most of the year we spend visiting in other people's houses, and it's not a very nice life. I can see Gran's point of view; she wants to see me settled. Only I've grown up quite a lot since last summer. I'm eighteen now and have seen more of the world and been to several parties although, of course, Gran can't afford to give me a Season in Town. I've learned to appreciate men who are prepared to devote their lives to the service of God.'

Frances was quick to pick up this hint. 'There is someone else . . .'

'That's my problem. Gran doesn't approve of my wishing to marry someone who is only a curate, though his second cousin dines with the Bishop twice a year, and we're sure that it's only a matter of time before Edwin gets a good living. But if I do accept Gavin's money, then I think Gran would agree that Edwin and I could get married straight away. Edwin could do so much good with the money, even if it did come from a man who . . . well, you know what he did.'

'Are you asking me for advice, Miss Seld? Or seeking approval of a course of action on which you have already decided?' Frances thought of the Will which had been discovered in Gavin Broome's Bible, the Will which left everything to Maud. She did not know what to say to Isabella. It was not her place to advise the girl. Shallow as Isabella undoubtedly was, Frances could pity her, knowing how false her hopes were of inheriting Gavin Broome's money. 'I suggest you consult with some member of your family; Mr Manning, for instance.' She withdrew her arm from Isabella's, and hurried after Agnes.

'No more confidences,' she said to herself. 'I cannot bear it.' But what it was she could not bear, she did not put into words.

*   *   *

Hugo removed his cigar from his mouth. 'I am in a very delicate position here, you know.'

His uncle shivered and drew nearer to the fire. The two men were sitting in the gun-room which served not only as a smoking-room, but also as the estate office. In addition, it housed some of the smaller pieces from the Broome collection of antique weapons, although the greater part had long since been consigned to the cellars.

'This new Will,' said Hugo, who did not appear to feel the cold as his uncle did, 'seems to be perfectly in order, although naturally we must have the opinion of the family solicitors on it. Will you break the news to Isabella?'

'I would rather wait until Mr Cotton has had a look at it,' said Mr Manning. Mr Cotton was the family solicitor, and his office was in Lewes. 'It's Gavin's signature all right, but somehow . . .'

'You would like to know why Gavin left nothing to his brother and to his servant under this new Will? I doubt if we will ever know. I suppose he may have cut Richard out of his Will because his brother didn't back him up over that scandalous affair of the woman Jervis. Perhaps Benson is not quite the devoted servant he pretends to be. Who

58

knows?'

'Gavin said nothing to me about changing his Will when he stayed with us last summer, and he was with us right up to the day he sailed back to South Africa. I can understand his wishing to cut Isabella out of his Will after the way she let him down, but . . . we talked freely on so many other subjects . . . I would have expected him to have mentioned the matter to me if . . .'

'It's plain that he changed his mind about leaving the money to Isabella after he got back to South Africa. The new Will is quite recent—early in February—after Richard's death. Although, of course, at the time he could not have known of his brother's death. It is all in order. I repeat: Isabella ought to be told, and you seem to me to be the person best qualified to break the news to her.'

Mr Manning sighed. He had a monkey-like face with luxuriant whiskers. He divided his time between charitable concerns and his own large family. He reflected that if Gavin had wanted to throw his money around, he might at least have thrown some in the way of his uncle's charities, or even in the way of his uncle's children. Why should everything have gone to Maud, whom Gavin had never liked? Why not equally to Maud and Agnes, if he had wanted to leave the money in the family? Gavin had always been fond of Agnes and deplored the fact that the child was alternately

59

petted and neglected. It was a puzzle.

Hugo placed a solid white hand over his uncle's. 'You are a great comfort to me, in this difficult time. You will speak to Isabella? Maud already knows.' A conscious look came over his face. 'I really think that Isabella ought to be told at once.'

'Very well,' said Mr Manning. 'I will tell her.' He threw another log on the fire, which began to smoke. He wished he were safely back in London, with his wife and children. Poor Rosalie! With three of the younger children down with measles, she had been unable to come with him . . . 'Damn this chimney! When do you think it was swept last?'

'In the days of old King William, I should think,' said Hugo. 'There is much that needs to be done.' He made a note with a gold pencil which had belonged to Richard. 'Chimneys,' he said, as he wrote the word down on his list. 'If only I could get on with it. This hanging around doesn't suit me.'

'Dr Kimpton said Gavin might linger a while, like his brother. A tough race, the Broomes, but Gavin was badly beaten around the head and his arm is in a bad way. Did you hear that Dr Kimpton is poorly today, and may not be able to come up? Don't you think we should call in a doctor from London? Gavin can afford it, if anyone can.'

Hugo pursed his lips. 'Let the beggar die

in peace, I say. What's the point of having him pulled about and submitted to all sorts of painful treatment, just to be up to date? If Dr Kimpton takes to his bed, his nephew will see Gavin out. And you know what we decided about the nursing.'

He was sitting at the bureau which housed all Richard's papers. 'I want to show you Miss Chard's references, if I can find them.' He searched through various drawers, picked up the new Will, read it, smiled, and locked it away.

'That money my aunt spoke of,' he said, still searching. 'Fifty guineas. Didn't she say that Richard used to keep a float of that sum in one of these drawers, and that she hasn't touched it since his death? I could do with some ready cash, but I can't find it. Maud says she hasn't had it, either, so it must be one of the servants. I really don't wish to call in the police. The servants are upset enough as it is, what with Gavin's returning, and having to adjust to two new masters in such a short period of time ... Did you hear that the family ghost has been seen again in the Cloisters? What nonsense will they think up next!'

'It will be Gavin's batman who is responsible for the rumours, I expect. He's half off his head with worry and fatigue, and sees murderers lurking in every shadow. A bad influence on the rest of the servants. No, I agree, we don't want to bring the police in.

Fifty guineas may seem a great sum to you at the moment, but it is a trifle compared to what Maud will inherit. Be patient; you will soon have enough money to do whatever you wish with the Court.'

Hugo flushed. He had been working as secretary to an out-of-office politician when he had been summoned to Furze Court. His salary had not been large and he had hated the work. His letter of resignation had gone off in the post the day he arrived at the Court.

The clock struck eleven, and the gentlemen checked their watches.

'I asked them to meet us in the hall at eleven,' said Hugo. 'Shall we go? By the way, I'm having the agent repair that footbridge over the river. Nothing has been done to repair it since . . . several of the struts are rotten. You can almost believe Gavin's story when you look at it.'

Mrs Broome was reclining on a settee in front of the fire in the Great Hall when they entered, and beside her sat Lady Amelia. Mr Manning paused to greet the ladies, but Hugo strode to the fireplace and stood with his back to it. The butler ushered Miss Chard into the room.

'Good morning, Miss Chard. My aunt has something to say to you. Aunt?'

'I'm so bad at explaining things, Hugo. Won't you . . .?'

Hugo needed no further prompting. 'Miss

Chard, as you may have perceived, we are in some difficulty as regards supervision of the sick-room. Mrs Broome is not well. Neither Miss Broome nor Miss Seld feel they can undertake the responsibility and, in short, we must ask you to take over the job until such time as . . . well, you understand me, I think?'

CHAPTER THREE

IT WAS done, and she was to nurse a man suspected of murder. There was no getting out of it. She had tried to excuse herself on the grounds of having had no experience of nursing, but Lady Amelia and Mr Manning had overridden her protests. She was to have whichever members of the staff she chose to assist her. The butler and the housekeeper had already been informed that her authority in the sick-room was to be absolute. The remaining agency nurse was at her disposal, but the midwife had returned to the village. Her duties to Agnes would be suspended until after the funeral; yes, Mr Manning had actually put it into words. Until after the funeral. He added in a kindly way that he thought she had worked wonders with young Agnes, and that the Broomes were very lucky to have her.

There was nothing for Miss Chard to do

but curtsey, and leave. At one and the same moment she wanted to burst into tears and resign her post, and to rush to the invalid's side. She was excited by her appointment, and feared the effect on her of close proximity to the sick man.

The Great Hall lay on the opposite side of the Court to the principal bedrooms. No one in his right senses would wish to cross the courtyard on such a day as this, with snow powdering the grass, so she turned to the right out of the Hall, to pass through the dining-room and music-room and thus gain the Oak Gallery on the south side of the Court.

Hugo Broome caught up with her as she entered the music-room. Servants were laying the table for lunch in the dining-room, but the music-room was deserted.

'The responsibility frightens you?' he asked, laying a large hand on her arm in familiar fashion. Frances shook her head. 'Ah, then you must have heard the rumours about my cousin? The inquest? The suspicions?'

'Such a thing ought not to make any difference to a nurse,' said Frances, thus betraying that it did, in fact, make a difference to her.

'Nevertheless, it is in the back of all our minds. I tell myself that perhaps a soldier might have looked on her death in a different light from a civilian. I have tried to find excuses for him, but . . .' He looked around.

The place was deserted. He drew her to one of the oriel windows. 'We are placing a great burden on you, Miss Chard. I am well aware of that. And, believe me, you will not find us ungrateful.'

'I hope I will always do my duty.'

'Perhaps there may be something required of you more than just doing your duty.' His expression conveyed a deeper, sinister meaning. 'There has been quite enough scandal attached to my cousin's name already. For his sake, and for the sake of his family, we would like the close of his life to be seemly. He must be well tended on his death-bed. That goes without saying. Dr Kimpton will help you, if he is well enough; but if not, the young doctor will do the trick. Although somehow I feel you will not need to call on him.'

Frances was puzzled. Was her imagination playing her tricks? Did he mean to insinuate . . .?

'You are intelligent, and resolute enough to do what has to be done.' Hugo's hand strayed up her arm to her shoulder. He cupped her chin in his hand, and tilted her face up to him. She could see his large white teeth coming closer. 'Too pretty to be a governess, aren't you? You've had some offers in your time, eh?'

She was afraid of this large man who seemed so sure of himself and of her. Would he kiss her? Surely not. Had she not seen with her own eyes that he was paying attentions to Maud? What would Maud think if she came in at that moment? Frances shivered. She thought she could guess exactly what Maud would say.

'You have no money of your own, I believe,' said Hugo. 'What a pity. With your background and education you ought to set up your own school one day. I am always looking out for possibilities of investing money—on a friend's behalf, of course. I am sure a school set up by you would repay any capital sum invested in it.'

She tried to laugh, to lighten the atmosphere. 'Oh, I have not been here long enough to justify . . .

'There are some services which can only be paid for with that kind of generosity. Think about it, Miss Chard.'

He left her, to return to the hall. Frances leaned against the window to recover. Had she understood him correctly? Had he tried to bribe her to ensure that Gavin Broome died under her hands? She remembered how Nurse Moon had been discovered lying on top of her patient, with a pillow over his face. Had Benson been right all along in suspecting foul play?

She pressed both hands to her temples and tried to think.

'Beg pardon, Miss,' someone said, close to her.

Frances jumped. One of the house-parlourmaids, little more than a child, stood before her. She had been crying. Frances' alarm dissolved, as it always would when her compassion was aroused.

'Sorry if I startled you, Miss. Only I'm that worried . . .' She sniffed and drew the back of her hand across her face. 'Have you seen a glass stopper anywhere, Miss? I've looked in all the bedrooms and the dining-room and even in the hall and the gun-room, but I can't see it anywhere. Mr Spilkins says that he's sure I've broken it and he's going to dock the money from my wages, and the bottle cost ever so much . . .'

Mr Spilkins was the butler.

'A cut-glass stopper, about so big?' Frances indicated the height of the object Agnes had found. The maid nodded. 'I may have seen it. You say it came from a decanter? Will you show me?'

'Not a decanter, Miss. From the desk set on the bureau, here. Sometimes Miss Seld takes it into her bedroom to write letters, but I've looked in her room, and I can't see it.'

Frances inspected the desk set. It was an ornate affair, complete with old-fashioned quill pens and two square, cut-glass ink bottles. One of the ink bottles had lost its stopper, but its fellow was similar in appearance to the one which Agnes had found on the floor of the sick-room.

'Miss Agnes found it,' said Miss Chard. 'I know where it is now.'

'Oh, of course. Miss Agnes does love things that sparkle. A proper magpie, she is.'

'She thought it belonged to Lord Broome, and it has been left in the sick-room. I will see that it is returned for you. Don't worry.'

The little maid was profuse with her thanks. Miss Chard had saved her from disgrace and the loss of half of her salary. Her name was Polly Dowding; this was her first job, which her aunt—who was in the kitchens—had got for her. Anything that Miss Chard wanted, she would only have to ask, and Polly would do it for her.

'Even help in the sick-room?' Frances thought it might be useful to have someone whom she could trust to help her.

Polly gulped, and then nodded. 'Only you'll have to ask Mr Spilkins.'

Frances said that she would do so, and Polly went galloping off down the music-room. She stopped abruptly when she came to the double doors leading into the dining-room, opened one of them with caution, peered round the edge to see if the coast was clear, and then slid from sight.

Frances went the opposite way, through the anteroom to Mrs Broome's apartments, and thence to the Oak Gallery. Benson was there, sitting astride a chair outside the door of the State Bedroom. He was watching Agnes, who

68

had chalked a grid on the wooden floor and was playing hopscotch.

'Miss Chard, Miss Chard!' Agnes came flying up and gave her governess a hug. 'Isn't it heavenly that I'm to have a holiday? Arling is to take me and Nurse to the Armstrongs and I'm to stay for two whole days and nights and play with their puppies and ride on their pony if it stops snowing. Oh, I'm so happy!'

Arling was the head groom, and the Armstrongs were a local family of importance, who lived about two miles away. Frances remembered Isabella had spoken of Miss Susan Armstrong, who would have liked to marry Gavin Broome. Before Frances could comment, Agnes had danced back to her game, and was absorbed in throwing a button into square number three.

Frances wondered if 'two days and nights' were supposed to see the end of Lord Broome, and fear trickled down her back. She put up her hand to smooth her hair, and sighed.

'That's right, Miss. We've got a lot to think about. I'm glad you're taking charge, for it's all got too much for me. One nurse, that's all we've got left, and she's not much use. She's away gossiping in the servants' hall now. Did you hear about the midwife? We've lost her, that's for certain.'

'No, I . . . what about Lord Broome? How is he?'

'Remember to call him "Major", Miss. He's

69

asleep. He wakes and eats and drinks and then dozes off again. He's going on all right. Do you want to see him? I don't mind your having a peep.'

'Not if he's asleep.' She did not want to see him at all, but could hardly say so to Benson. 'What was that about the midwife?'

'She said she saw the family ghost. I don't hold with ghosts, no more than the Major ever did. Of course, I've heard him tell the story about there being an abbey here once and that one of the monks was supposed to walk the Cloisters when the head of the house was in danger. It made a good story, the way he used to tell it. But this is different.' He kept his voice low, watching Agnes at play.

'Mrs Peach saw the ghost?'

'I didn't say that. She saw something or somebody dressed up as a monk. At first I thought she'd dreamed it, but she's conscientious enough, and she keeps herself awake in the night by knitting. I saw how much she'd done to her knitting between the time I went to bed and the time she woke me up with her screeching, and I reckon she'd been awake all right, and working away at her needles. I was sleeping on my cot, and she was sitting by the Major's bed. She said she looked up and saw something big and white reflected in the pier-glass in the dressing-room. She thought at first it was me, so she got up quiet-like, and went to the door between the two rooms, and

70

saw someone standing in the dressing-room doorway, here. The one that's always locked. So she screamed. Luckily you gave the Major that sleeping draught, or he'd have heard her. By the time I got myself awake there wasn't anything to be seen. The door was locked, just as it has been ever since I got here. She was gathering her things together. She said she wasn't paid to put up with ghosts and that she was going straight home. I said she couldn't leave the house at night, because the outside doors would be locked. She said she didn't care, she'd sleep in a chair in the servants' hall if she had to, but she wasn't stopping here. So I said good riddance, and put a chair under the knob of both doors, and went back to sleep. Only, we won't get anyone else to come up from the village to give us a hand, because she'll have told the story to everyone by now.'

Frances pressed her hand to her forehead. 'I don't understand. You say you don't believe in ghosts, and that the door was still locked, yet you put chairs under the knobs of both doors . . .?'

He glanced down the Gallery. Agnes had abandoned her game and run off. He beckoned Frances to the locked dressing-room door, and tried the handle. He indicated that Frances should do so, too. The door was still locked. Then Benson set his finger against the keyhole and brought it away smeared with some dark substance. Frances followed his

71

example.

'That's oil, Miss. Someone's oiled that lock and the hinges of the door, too. You could slip a key in and turn it as easily as if the lock were fitted yesterday. You could swing that door open without a whisper of sound. Ghosts don't need to use oil on the locks of doors, do they?'

Frances smelt and tasted the stuff on her finger. Benson was right. It was oil.

'I think someone's got hold of the key to this door, Miss, and maybe he's got the key to the bedroom door, too. I think someone came in by this dressing-room door last night, dressed up in some monkish gown or other. When that midwife saw them, they took fright, closed and locked the door and ran away.'

'But why? What does it all mean?'

'It means just what it's supposed to mean, Miss. It means that the head of the House of Broome is in danger.'

A faint cry came from the sick-room.

'Don't forget to call him "Major",' said Benson again, as he followed Frances into the sick-room. Lord Broome was trying to raise himself from his pillows. He was not only conscious, but he knew who Benson was. He reached out his right hand to his batman, smiling, and trying to utter his name. The second time he got it right.

'Why, Major!' Benson's voice was as indistinct as his master's, but for a different reason. Frances busied herself with a rearrangement of the window curtains.

'Home?' said the sick man. His eyes went round the room. They stopped at Frances. He frowned, as if unsure where he'd seen her before. 'Richard,' he said. 'Where's Richard? This is his room . . . his bed. Not here?'

'He's in London,' gabbled Benson, giving the first excuse that came into his head. He picked up a basin of water but, made clumsy by emotion, spilt some on the coverlet. Frances took the basin and flannel off Benson and washed the sick man's face and hands. Lord Broome's eyes narrowed, observing her, but she did not speak, and neither did he. She knew that her colour was rising. She knew that she ought to say something—anything— make some commonplace remark about the weather, or . . . anything to break the silence which was beginning to be significant. Yet she could think of nothing to say.

'It's Miss Chard, Major,' said Benson. 'She's been put in charge, while you're ill. Your aunt's not feeling too good at the moment, and . . .'

'I remember you,' said Lord Broome, speaking to Frances. 'Nightmares . . . and then you came.' He frowned. Evidently his memory was still imperfect. 'Singing?' he asked, more in doubt that he had his facts right than as if he remembered what had happened exactly.

'Are you hungry?' said Frances, keeping her voice matter-of-fact. 'Do you want anything?

How do you feel?'

Before they could prevent him, Lord Broome had removed his left arm from the sling which Theo had put round his neck, and experimentally leaned on it. Gasping with pain, he fell back on his pillows. 'As bad as ever,' he said.

'It would be, Major,' said Benson, moving towards the door. 'I'll fetch Dr Kimpton. You've got a bullet in your arm that's got to come out.'

Lord Broome raised his good hand. 'Not that old woman. His hands shake. He'd hack me to death. Tell Richard. Telegraph him. A specialist from London.'

'That will all take time,' said Frances. 'Benson, send for Dr Green. He can decide whether we should telegraph to London for a second opinion or not.'

'I'd forgotten that Theo would be qualified by now.' The sick man's eyelids were sinking already. Frances held a glass of water to his lips and he drank. There was sweat on his forehead, and he breathed shallowly, trying to master the pain in his arm.

'What shall I do?' Benson hovered in the doorway.

'Do as the Colonel says,' instructed Lord Broome.

Frances laughed at Benson's bewilderment. 'He means me,' she explained. 'I'm the Colonel.'

'Yes,' said the sick man. 'I remember you.'
And he smiled, too.

*   *   *

It was a dead hour in the day. In the gun-room
Hugo and his uncle were puzzling over the
dates on Miss Chard's references. Maud was
going through her wardrobe with her maid
Meakins. Isabella was writing a letter to her
curate while her grandmother slept. Agnes was
sorting out a collection of things for Nurse to
pack, ready for her visit to the Armstrongs.

The butler dozed at his post in the pantry.
This was at the foot of the servants' staircase,
at the side of the gun-room. From this vantage
point Spilkins was supposed to be able to keep
an eye on everything that happened at the
Court, and, to give him his due, he usually did
know where every member of the family might
happen to be at any given time. Benson found
him in his usual chair, and asked that someone
be sent to the village for Dr Green, urgently.

'The doctor's in with Mrs Broome,' said
Spilkins. 'She's had another attack. Glauber's
salts, that's what she ought to take. Mrs
Spilkins swore by them, when she was alive.'
He rang a bell, and Polly appeared. 'The
doctor's wanted in the State Bedroom. Wait
for him outside Mrs Broome's apartments, and
tell him when he comes out.'

The access to the tower apartments was

75

through an anteroom at the junction of the Oak Gallery and the music-room, so back went Benson, with Polly chattering at his side.

'I hope the doctor's won't be long,' said Polly. 'There's company coming for tea. The Armstrongs are coming to fetch Miss Agnes and Nurse away, and the vicar is coming because he wants to see Lord Broome, and Dr Green is coming back to fetch Dr Kimpton because the old man's not fit to ride in this weather.'

'But Dr Green is with Mrs Broome now, isn't he?'

'Not he! She wouldn't have him at any price. He won't waste time buttering her up, that's why.'

Benson was beginning to explain that he didn't want to see Dr Kimpton when the latter appeared, with Mrs Broome on his arm.

'Ah, Polly,' said Mrs Broome. 'Will you find Meakins for me at once?' Meakins acted as maid to both mother and daughter. 'I have mislaid my diamond bracelet, the one dear Richard gave me to mark his engagement to Maud. The catch was loose, I know. You haven't seen it, by any chance?'

'No, Ma'am. Meakins is with Miss Maud, Ma'am. I'll fetch her. And please, Ma'am, the doctor's wanted in the sick-room.'

'My poor nephew,' said Mrs Broome. 'Worse, is he? Doctor, you will join us for tea in the hall when you have seen Gavin? I did

76

mean to drop in on him this morning, but my head . . .'

Rapid footsteps announced the approach of Theo Green, come to fetch his uncle. He bowed to Mrs Broome. 'Mrs Broome, I've just heard in the village about Mrs Peach. I'm afraid I can't persuade her to return. Would you like us to telegraph for another nurse from the agency in Lewes?'

'I leave all that sort of thing to Miss Chard. She will know what to do for the best. Dear Dr Kimpton; your arm as far as the hall? I feel I would be happier with someone to lean on, after that attack . . . and you really ought to take something for that cold of yours.'

The elder doctor was leaning against the panelling, trying to smother a cough. 'Delighted . . . tea would be delightful . . . Theo, one minute . . . his lordship has to be visited . . .'

Benson pulled on Theo's sleeves. 'There's been a misunderstanding. It's you that's wanted to see the Major, but the servants thought your uncle . . .'

'That's right. He's in charge of the case. Uncle, you should be in bed. I brought the trap for you.'

Polly whispered in Benson's ear that perhaps Miss Chard could persuade the young doctor to take the case since everyone knew that Dr Green was sweet on the governess.

'Is he, now?' said Benson to himself.

'My bracelet . . .' said Mrs Broome, distractedly. She gave a ladylike little cough. 'Gracious, but it is cold out here. There should be a good fire in the Great Hall. Doctor, your arm? Positively, you must stay for tea. I won't take "no" for an answer. You can always see Gavin afterwards. I am sure there can't be the least hurry in the matter. Sinking fast, I believe. Very sad. Polly, tell Meakins to look for my bracelet. Dr Green, I suppose you will take a cup of tea with us while you are waiting for your uncle?'

Doors along the Gallery were opening to disgorge members of the family, ready for the ritual of tea. They went off together, doctors and all. The ghostly cross chalked on the floorboards by Agnes earlier that day reminded Benson of the "monk's' visit. He shivered. What with the indifference of the Broome family to his lordship's sufferings, and the apathy of the servants, he felt as if he were shouting for help in a foreign language which no one understood.

Miss Chard came out of the sick-room. He told her what had happened. He saw that she thought he had not tried hard enough to get the young doctor. He felt defeated. 'It's a matter of etiquette,' he tried to excuse himself and Theo. 'He can't take on his uncle's case.'

'Nonsense,' said Miss Chard. 'You men are all the same. Etiquette, indeed! I'll give him etiquette, when I see him.'

'If you would have a word with him, Miss?'

Meakins, the black-clad ladies' maid, interrupted them. With her pinched features and flat body, she was not a prepossessing figure, but she was devoted to Maud and, to a lesser extent, also to Mrs Broome.

'Madam has mislaid her diamond bracelet,' said Meakins to Miss Chard. 'Have you seen it anywhere, Miss Chard?' Her manner verged on the insolent, as if she were implying that the governess had stolen the bracelet. Miss Chard shook her head and said the bracelet would probably turn up. Meakins hesitated as if she would like to say something else, and then turned on her heel and walked off. She had a curious, gliding walk, which made it appear as if she moved on wheels.

'Good riddance,' said Benson, more or less under his breath as Meakins disappeared. 'I can't abide that woman. She's probably stolen it herself. And the money that's missing from the gun-room. Did you hear about that, Miss? They're full of it, in the servants' hall. Though from what I've seen of this place, the money could have gone at any time since Mr Richard was killed. They're a careless lot around here. I asked if anyone had seen anything of our monkish visitor. Several of them said they had, but not since Mr Richard died. They seemed to think Mrs Peach saw one of the footmen who is courting Polly Dowding, because he was out of his quarters last night, late. He says he went to fetch some apples from the winter store for her, and that though he went through the Cloisters, he didn't go anywhere near the Gallery. Spilkins ought to have stopped the lad. The discipline here is terrible.'

'Abel wouldn't lie,' said someone in a small voice behind them. It was Polly, and her cheeks were suspiciously red. 'Really he wouldn't, Miss Chard!'

'I believe you,' said Frances. 'Run along and fetch Dr Green for me, will you, Polly? He'll be having tea in the hall with the others. You needn't let them know what I want him for.'

*   *   *

Theo was enjoying himself. When not exercising his calling, he liked to watch other people, and try to guess at the motives which lay behind their behaviour. To him, Mrs Broome was an uninteresting, selfish woman, who neglected her intelligent but gawky younger daughter to lavish attention on Maud. Of course Miss Broome was beautiful, but she was also proud and hard. At this very moment Mrs Broome was trying unsuccessfully to attract Maud's attention, while Maud had eyes for no one but Hugo, and was refusing to heed the signals her mother was sending her. Now what was that all about?

Lady Amelia was stonewalling Mrs Armstrong's questions about how long "dear Gavin' might be expected to last. The Armstrongs were worth a study in themselves; the General so upright, so distinguished, and so very much under the thumb of his diminutive lady. Mrs Armstrong was the uncrowned queen of the county and very conscious of her position. It was she who had been responsible for Gavin Broome's ostracism after the inquest on Lilien Jervis, and it was she who was now loudest in condemning the police because they had so far failed to find the men who attacked him on the train.

Mr Manning and Isabella were sitting close together on the far side of the fire. It looked to Theo as if the girl had been crying. Mr Manning seemed to be trying to protect the girl from the prying eyes of the rest of the company. Why?

Polly slipped into the hall and stopped at Theo's elbow. Could he spare a moment to speak with Miss Chard? It was urgent. Yes, Theo could always spare a moment to speak with Miss Chard. He abandoned his study of human nature to follow Polly to the Gallery.

'At last,' said Miss Chard. 'Your bag! Where is it? You brought it with you?'

'In the trap, but . . .'

Frances sent Polly for the doctor's bag, and explained rapidly but concisely why she had sent for him. Theo protested that he could not possibly offend his uncle by taking over Lord

Broome's case. She insisted that Lord Broome did not wish to see Dr Kimpton, and had asked for Theo by name.

'You could always manage your uncle, if you chose,' said Miss Chard. 'He is not at all well, I understand. You could say you wished to save him the trouble of a routine call, just as you did last night. Or, if you prefer it, lay all the blame on me.'

'I could not blame you for anything,' said Theo. He took her hand. She looked startled, and the quick colour rushed into her face. She withdrew her hand, with a sharp movement which he interpreted as a rebuff. Theo had not until that moment realised that he loved Miss Chard. He went over his financial position in his mind; if his uncle were to retire, he could afford to marry quite soon. If Polly had not at that moment come running with his bag, he might have proposed to Frances, then and there.

'You will remember not to call him by his title?' said the object of his affections, her hand on the bedroom door. 'He appears to be getting stronger all the time, but I am sure he is not yet ready to bear the shock of his brother's death. All the servants have been warned . . . but I am so afraid that a momentary lapse on the part of one of them might tell him the truth.'

There was a rustle of cloth somewhere behind them, and a door closed softly. Frances exchanged glances with Theo, and they went into the sick-room. There was no privacy in that house.

'Theo!' Lord Broome sat up and extended his good hand, smiling.

'Why, old fellow—here's a thing!' A rush of affection made Theo cling to his patient's hand even as his doctor's reflexes absorbed the fact that his patient's temperature was slightly up, and his eye too bright for perfect health. The agency nurse was sitting, sewing, by the window. Theo signed to her to assist him in making an examination, but Frances was there already, drawing back the bed-covers.

'I came in last night to see how you were,' said Theo, 'but you were asleep.'

'I seem to have missed a lot,' observed Lord Broome. 'The nurse tells me it is Palm Sunday, and yet that's snow falling outside, if I'm not mistaken. The last thing I remember clearly is the bad weather in the Bay of Biscay.'

'You don't remember how you came by the bullet in your arm, or those bumps on the head?' Theo lifted his head to ask the nurse to bring a lamp, and there was Frances, already lighting one for him.

'Won't you enlighten me?'

It was Frances who replied, saying that he had been attacked and robbed coming home in the train from Lewes. His lordship frowned.

'Did the police get anyone for it?'

'No, not yet. You don't remember your

assailants?'

'Trying to remember makes my head ache.'

Theo diverted him by asking for a full account of how he had come by the original injury to his arm. The nurse unwound the bandages, but it was Frances who helped the sick man move to one side of the bed so that Theo could inspect his injuries.

'There's been a truce since, hasn't there?' said Lord Broome. 'Yes, of course. I tell you, if ever we're forced to fight against the Boers again, we'll be up against it. We have nothing as good as their rifles, and you can't see them in their dun-coloured farm clothes; we're sitting ducks in scarlet. It was at Majuba. January 29th. We had to charge up the hill at them. They picked off the officers, or went for our horses. Good strategy. My horse was hit and as I felt him begin to go down, Summers swerved across my path. He'd been hit, too. We went down in a heap, me swearing, the horses lashing out . . . I felt the pain in my forearm, and I thought: What luck! To be struck by my own horse . . . sharp as a razor, across the inside of my arm. I can remember thinking that I'd better get a tourniquet on it quickly, or I'd bleed to death . . . then . . . I can't remember . . . they say I walked back to camp, carrying Summers . . . He died, poor fellow . . . more died of fever than from their wounds . . .'

His breath hissed softly between his teeth as

84

Theo turned the mutilated arm this way and that. After a minute or two, he went on.

'When I came to myself again, I was on board ship, with my arm in splints. They said I'd got to see some quack or other in London about my arm, because it wasn't right. The bone was broken. They set it, but . . .'

Theo bent the limp thumb and first finger. 'Any feeling or movement?'

'Not yet. Give me a chance. When the splints come off . . .' His voice tailed away, as if it had only just dawned on him that the splints were already off. 'When you've taken the bullet out, it will be all right.' He seemed to dare Theo to disagree.

Theo's face gave nothing away. He began to touch his patient's elbow with the tips of his fingers. The bullet was still in the arm, they knew, but they did not know precisely where. His uncle had probed for it unsuccessfully, as had the doctor from Lewes, but this was the first time that Theo had been allowed access to the wound. There was as yet no sign of infection.

His lordship's teeth grated together. Theo stopped probing. He rebandaged the forearm, and then beckoned Frances to follow him from the room.

'No, you don't,' said his lordship, preventing Frances from leaving by the simple expedient of laying hold of her dress. 'You stay here. It's my arm, and I want to hear what you plan to

85

do with it.'

'There's no cause for alarm,' said Theo, too hurriedly for conviction.

'I'll tell you what he's going to say,' said Lord Broome. 'Open wounds ask for trouble, and if he—or somebody else—doesn't dig that bullet out and sew up the wound, gangrene will set in, and I'll die. On the other hand, if the bullet is lodged high in the forearm, it's going to be the very devil to dig it out without doing a lot of damage, which in turn might necessitate amputation. He doesn't think I'm strong enough to stand either a long operation or an amputation, and there he's probably right.'

'I was going to suggest sending for my late chief from London. He's a fine surgeon.'

There was silence while his lordship appeared to look at and then through Theo. 'No,' he said at last. 'Let's get it over and done with. You do it, and do it now. Get the bullet out, sew it up, and I'll be on my feet again tomorrow. Leave it, and I'll be dead in a week. Give me something to bite on, and I'll not complain.'

'Impossible. I have no anaesthetic with me for a start, and . . .'

'No ether or chloroform for me. What? Do you think I can't stand a little pain? Besides, if you know I'm watching you, you'll be quick. Once the bullet is out, the rest will be easy, and maybe my thumb . . .' To emphasise his point, he tried to sit up, unwarily moved his bad arm and gasped with pain.

'He is not fit,' said Theo to Frances. 'I could not take the risk. I will get Mr Manning to telegraph to London for Sir Stanley Ellis, and in the meantime my patient must be kept quiet. No visitors, no excitement, no alcohol, and a plain diet. He's game enough, but he's been much weakened by what he's been through.' It seemed Theo was right, for his lordship made no further plea for an immediate operation.

Theo held the door open for Frances, but his lordship called her back.

'Where's my shawl?'

'It's on the bed. But it's not yours. It's mine. Benson can find you something else.'

'Nothing else suits me as well.'

'My wardrobe is limited; I only have two shawls, that grey one, and a black one for evening. My black one is not warm enough for this weather.'

'Benson: send to Lewes for a selection of shawls for the Colonel. Any colour except grey, which doesn't suit her.'

Now Frances invariably wore grey in the day-time. 'I protest,' she said, overriding Theo's request to know who "the Colonel" might be. 'I could not possibly accept such a gift from you.'

'Aren't I old enough to be your father?'

Before she had given herself time to think

where this line of talk might lead, Frances had blurted out that she would be four-and-twenty in June.

'There, now!' said his lordship. 'And I was convinced you must be at least twenty-five.'

Out-manoeuvred, Frances left the room, and it cannot be said that her exit was noiseless. Theo gazed at the door which she had slammed in his face, and the green demon of jealousy took possession of him.

'Miss Chard is a most estimable young woman,' he said. 'You ought not to trifle with her.'

'What! You, too? Oh, Theo . . . what a tangle!'

*   *   *

The news that Lord Broome had recovered consciousness was received by his family and the staff at the Court with consternation, quickly soothed by the rider that he required an immediate and difficult operation on his arm. After the news had been discussed in all its aspects before, during and after dinner, it was agreed that the situation had not altered materially in any way. Theo had taken his uncle home after tea, but his subdued account of the pros and cons of the operation, reinforced by his air of depression, had convinced Mr Manning and Hugo that Gavin's death was still only a matter of time.

Frances made arrangements for Polly and another of the housemaids to help the agency nurse and Benson in the sickroom, and retired to her own quarters. She was mentally worn out, and ill-prepared to meet the crisis which arose that evening. She was not required to dine with the family that night, and so was having supper on a tray in the schoolroom when Polly burst in with the demand that she "Come, quick!" 'The Reverend's in the sickroom, praying over Lord Broome something awful! He said the wrath of God would light on me if I interfered with him in the path of his duty, and that he's settling down for a long struggle for Lord Broome's soul; and Lord Broome's not asleep, though he's pretending he is . . .'

Long before the two women reached the Gallery, they could hear the divine's sonorous voice, raised in prayer.

'Fit to wake the dead,' said Polly, with a nervous giggle. 'I thought of going for Mr Benson, but he's in Mr Arling's cottage for the evening, and you were nearer. Did I do right?'

'Absolutely. Lord Broome must be kept quiet.' Polly had left the sick-room door half-open in her flight. Frances went in, and shut it behind her. The man of God was on his knees, his eyes closed, and his knuckles white as he exhorted Lord Broome to repent.

'. . . in the day that you stand before the tribunal of God . . .'

Frances looked at the man on the bed, and agreed with Polly that he was awake; there was an awareness in the room when he was awake which was easy to identify. She waited till the vicar paused to draw breath, and touched him on the shoulder.

'Too kind . . . too good of you . . . How I wish we hadn't given him so much laudanum tonight! What a pity that he cannot hear you and receive the benefit of your efforts!'

'Begone, woman! I must wrestle with this man's soul tonight, before it is too late, and he is gone from us for ever, into damnation everlasting!'

'Should I try to wake him for you? I fear I would not succeed, but . . . your prayers for his recovery are so valuable . . .'

'If he should die before . . .'

'Quite so. But as he is unconscious and unable to hear you, would it not be of more value to gather around you one or two members of his family and household, so that you could all pray together?'

The vicar paused. There was something very appealing in the idea of holding an impromptu service at the Court. The Great Hall, moreover, had acoustics infinitely superior to those of the sick-room. He rose to his feet.

'Too cruel to bring you out on a night such as this,' said Frances, exerting all her charm while leading him to the door.

'I cannot think of my own bodily weakness

at such a time. I will come again in the morning. Perhaps the doctor can be informed that I wish to speak to him before the operation. He must be brought to repent, before . . .'

'I entirely agree with you. Polly, see our guest to the hall, will you?'

She returned to the sick-room, shut the door and leaned against it. Her sigh of relief was echoed from the bed.

'A brilliant piece of strategy, Colonel; boldly conceived and well carried out. I shall see that you are mentioned in my next despatch to the Home Office.'

She busied herself about the room, making him comfortable for the night.

'Richard?' he asked. 'They have telegraphed to him? Maud is with him in London, I assume. She always wanted him to hire a house in Town for her. Is she breeding yet? Is that why he hasn't come back to see me?'

'We have telegraphed to London,' said Frances, purposely misleading him. 'And we hope the surgeon will arrive by the first train in the morning.'

'Charter a special train, if necessary.' He was restless. She rearranged his pillows, wondering whether Theo had thought of chartering a special. She rather thought he had not, and wondered why. She asked him how he felt, and he said that he was better, but there was a flush on his cheek that she did not like.

91

She held his wrist, trying to feel his pulse. He pulled his hand away, mocking her.

'I don't think you know how to take a pulse, do you?' She blushed. She did not. 'Shall I tell you how I am? My headache has gone. I can think clearly, and see clearly, and hear clearly. I feel very tired, but that is nothing. Weakness, merely. I have a slight fever, and my arm bums. However, the bandages don't feel too tight, so there is no inflammation as yet. You see, I have more experience of wounds and nursing than you.' He turned his head, listening. 'Something is wrong, here. The house doesn't feel or sound right. Perhaps my hearing is not yet . . . no, it's far too quiet. There's no noise of the dogs in the courtyard, or servants laughing.'

He was very quick, she thought. She must be on her guard. He must not learn the truth about his brother before he had the operation.

'It has been snowing heavily. No one goes into the courtyard at the moment if they can help it. Now, please: no more questions. Suppose I gave you an answer which upset you . . . suppose I informed you that your favourite mare was lame, or that someone you dislike is occupying the bedchamber in which you usually sleep, or some other disaster of world-shattering proportions? You would work yourself into a state, and be unable to sleep, and then what would Dr Green say to me in the morning?'

'I am not a child.'

'No, and because of that, I want you to refrain from asking questions on unimportant matters. Concentrate on getting through the operation. That's an order from the Colonel, if you want it that way. When you are feeling better, I will gossip with you to your heart's content.'

'I am feeling better, but I see what you mean. I agree to your terms, if you will promise me something in return. If the surgeon doesn't arrive tomorrow morning, will you make Theo do the operation? I ought to have insisted that he did it today.'

'He is the doctor, after all. He ought to know what to do for the best. You talk as if he were not to be trusted.'

'He isn't. Not now.'

She wanted to say that she didn't know what he meant, but she rather thought that she did, and therefore said nothing.

'And if I go off my head with fever,' he said, 'you'll forgive me if I happen to use the odd swear-word or two? I would not wish to offend you by swearing, but I've lived most of my life abroad and in the company of men. I believe I have a reputation for ripe language.'

'I promise I will be deaf.'

'Cross your heart and hope to die?' He held out his good hand, and she shook it. He sank into an uneasy doze. In half an hour he was awake, looking round in a puzzled way

93

as if unsure where he might be. She soothed him, gave him a sleeping draught, and felt her nerves tighten as his hand touched hers. She was sure he was too hot for health.

When Polly came to relieve her, Lord Broome was sound asleep, and it was ten o'clock. Frances touched his hand. He did not stir. She thought him a little less hot than he had been. He did not stir even when Polly gave Frances an account of how funny the family and household had looked, all on their knees in the Great Hall while the vicar prayed at them, and all of them dying to get to their beds.

As Frances went up the stairs to her own bed, she was thinking of Lord Broome, and of the murder that he was supposed to have committed. Suppose Lilien's death had been an accident, as Gavin Broome had maintained; what of that? What if the woman had become pregnant by someone at the Court? There were more than two dozen active, able-bodied men employed there, and why should it have been Gavin Broome who had been responsible for her condition? Why could it not have been Richard Broome, instead?

No, she reflected, it could not have been Richard. He had been engaged to Maud at the time, and, anyway, he had a reputation for being shy of women. She had heard it said that he had never looked a woman in the face until he proposed to Maud, and certainly what she had seen of him bore that out.

Well, if not Richard or Gavin Broome, why not one of the footmen? Or one of the grooms? Lilien had gone to Gavin Broome when she had been thrown out by her husband; well, why not? Who else should she have gone to for help but a member of the Broome family? She would have known that neither Mrs Broome nor Maud would be sympathetic, and that Richard was always short of money. Yes, it would have been only natural for her to approach Gavin for help.

And then the clinching argument. Lord Broome had feared to distress her by using bad language if he became delirious, but he had said nothing about fearing to betray knowledge of murder.

'Which proves,' said Frances to herself, 'that he is no murderer. Doesn't it?'

CHAPTER FOUR

Frances had to break the ice in her water-jug next morning. She set her teeth so that they should not chatter with cold while she dressed. The fire in the schoolroom had not been lit that morning, and the nurseries were dark and silent with both Agnes and Nurse away.

Frances did not feel any the better for her night's rest; as soon as she got into bed she had begun to speculate on the relationship between Gavin Broome and his cousin Maud. Maud had been engaged to marry Richard before Gavin returned to South Africa, so why had Gavin chosen to leave all his money to Maud? Frances could understand his disinheriting Isabella, but the only reason she could think of why he should leave his money to Maud was that there had been an 'understanding' between Gavin and Maud, before Maud's engagement to Richard. At that time Richard had the title and the estate, and would be the more eligible suitor of the two. Perhaps Gavin had then turned to Isabella on the rebound and, when Isabella proved worthless, had left all his money to his first love, Maud. Frances was unable to fault her theory. It would explain much. It would even explain why the second Will left nothing to Richard. Richard was a spendthrift; if Gavin left his money to Maud, she would be able to look after it for Richard.

Having found a solution to the puzzle of the two Wills ought to have given Frances an untroubled night's sleep, but it had not done so. In the eerie light which filtered through snow-powdered windows, Frances scolded her reflection in the mirror, as she brushed her hair.

'You are a fool! What if he does love his cousin Maud? Is she not beautiful, and accomplished, and well-born and his equal socially? When he learns of his brother's death—and he must, sooner or later—will his grief not be softened by the knowledge that Maud is still free?' Her brush caught on a tangle of hair, and Miss Chard, that responsible, calm and intelligent governess, burst into tears.

Down in the village, Theo cut himself while shaving. He, too, had had a bad night. His uncle was worse, and had agreed to stay in bed that day. 'But take care how you go on at the Court,' said old Dr Kimpton, who was wise in the ways of the gentry. 'The patronage of the Broomes is worth several hundred pounds a year to a country doctor, and you don't want to be associated with the idea of failure at the beginning of your professional career. Let someone else take the responsibility for operating on his lordship. It's not likely that he will pull through, whatever you do, and it's better not to give them the chance to say he might have lived if you hadn't been so quick to use your knife.'

Be sure that Theo agreed with his uncle. Once he had been a champion of Gavin Broome's, but now he was full of doubts. Lilien had been a beauty, and Gavin no more of a saint than any other man of his class. That he did not boast about his affairs of the heart did not prove he had had none.

Lilien had gone straight from her husband to Gavin Broome. He had given her money, and sent her to Lewes, where she had been seen living in some style right up to the day of her death. She had come back to the park to meet Gavin. It was anyone's guess how she had come to fall in the river. Gavin had sworn that he had spotted her while he was out riding in the park, that he had called out to her as she was about to step on the bridge, that she had turned sharply, startled by his voice, had caught her foot, fallen against one of the handrails, that the rotten wood had snapped and precipitated her into the river. Gavin had said that he had gone in after her without success, that she had risen to the surface further down the river, and that by the time he got her out she was dead. No one could prove that it had happened otherwise. The coroner had returned a verdict of Misadventure, and the girl had been buried in the churchyard, which was more than some thought she had deserved. If the girl had not been known to be pregnant, or if her father had not cursed the House of Broome as he threw earth on to his daughter's coffin; if Mrs Armstrong had not given a lead to the county by cutting Gavin dead; and if Isabella had only stood by her fiancé . . . if Miss Chard had only acted in as discreet a manner towards Lord Broome as she had done towards Theo . . .

There was the nub of the matter. Theo was an honest man and not practised in the act of self-deception. He told himself that he only had to abstain from operating, and his hands would be clean. If the surgeon arrived, well and good; the responsibility for Gavin's life or death would be passed to someone else. If the surgeon did not arrive, then he, Theo Green, must not be rushed into attempting such a difficult operation himself. No one would blame him. Except—possibly—himself.

Theo cut himself while shaving.

*   *   *

Benson was shaving his master when Frances arrived in the sick-room. Lord Broome seemed to Frances to be very little, if any, worse than on the previous night. He had eaten some breakfast, and was sitting upright instead of leaning against his pillows as before. Benson said that the agency nurse had not yet reported for duty, and that he was hanged if he could do everything himself. Frances and Lord Broome interpreted this to mean that Benson was worried about his master. Frances sent Benson off to find the nurse and also to ascertain when the London surgeon and Dr Green were due to arrive.

'Is Richard ill?' asked Lord Broome, when they were alone. 'I wish you'd tell me what's keeping him. He may be irresponsible and selfish, but he'd not let me down like this if he could help it.'

'Your brother is well enough where he is,'
99

said Frances, crossing her fingers within the folds of her gown. 'And he would not thank you for working yourself into a fever on his account.'

'I don't know what's the matter with everyone this morning. Benson behaves as if I can't be trusted to be left on my own for more than a minute, nurses come and go without a word of explanation, the house is as quiet as the grave, and you look as if you've been crying. Why?'

'A personal matter,' said Frances, and to avoid further conversation went through into the dressing-room and sat on Benson's cot. She could see Lord Broome in the mirror from there. He could see her, too. He lay watching her. He did not ask her to return. He looked better now that he'd been shaved, but very white and drawn. Presently he slid down on the pillows and dozed off. Frances bowed her head over her knees. She knew what ailed her: jealousy. Jealousy of Maud. She had thought once that she had loved Walter Donne; she knew now that she had never loved him, for she had never felt like this about him.

After some time she raised her head. She had come to a decision and would stick to it. If Gavin Broome loved his cousin Maud, and if Maud's presence might help him through the operation, then by hook or by crook Miss Chard was going to see to it that Maud presented herself in the sick-room without

100

delay.

Benson returned, causing the sick man to waken. The batman shook his head at Frances. 'The nurse is being sick all over the place. Eaten something to disagree with her, she says. Dr Green hasn't appeared yet. Arling went to the station to meet the train, but there's been no word from London from the surgeon to say he's coming.'

'Theo's going to scratch,' said Lord Broome. 'Remember what you promised, Colonel.'

Frances remembered. 'Benson, go and fetch Dr Green. Don't come back without him.'

Benson went. Frances pulled the bed-covers straight. She could not look her patient in the eye, but she could still command her voice. 'Would you like to see some member of your family while we are waiting?'

'My aunt, you mean? She'd be more likely to tell me about her own symptoms than ask about mine.'

'There's Lady Amelia . . .?'

'My poor godmother! This cold weather won't do her rheumatism any good. They always give her the Blue Bedroom and the chimney smokes.'

'Miss Seld?'

'You ought to know better than to ask. I'm sure that you do know better. I had a lucky escape there, didn't I?'

'Well, what about Miss Broome?'

'Agnes?' He smiled. 'She's a darling, but too

energetic for me at the moment. Later.'

'I mean Miss Maud Broome.'

There was a pause. 'You mean she and my brother did not marry, after all?'

'No, the marriage never took place. Would you like to see her?'

'Good grief, no. We've never got on, you know. So Richard got out of it, did he? No wonder he's fled the place. About the wisest thing he could do. She must be in a temper to end all tempers.'

'Oh!' cried Miss Chard. 'You don't care for her, then? Nor Miss Seld?'

'Maud is a shrew, and Isabella a fool. Don't tell me you haven't come to the same conclusion, for I wouldn't believe you.'

'It is not my place to go round forming opinions of either of your cousins.'

His lordship gave a shout of laughter. 'Oh, Frances—what a mixture of discretion and imprudence! Does your heart always lead your head? Now tell me. Why were you crying? Was it for Theo?'

'Of course not.'

'Are you going to have him?'

'Marry him, you mean? No, I am not.'

'Why not? He's young, able-bodied, ambitious, and he loves you.'

'Does he? Oh, I am sure he doesn't. No, I'm not going to marry him. He's not man enough for me. No, I didn't mean that, exactly.'

'Yes, you did.' Lord Broome was grinning,

and somehow had managed to catch hold of a fold of her dress. 'Well, will you have me, if I get through the operation in one piece?'

She had not been expecting it. The room went dark around her. She grasped the bedcurtain to steady herself. She took two slow breaths, in and out. 'What nonsense!' she said. Her voice broke. She took out her handkerchief and blew her nose. She went over to the mirror and started to push pins in and out of her hair. She made herself laugh. 'A joke is a joke, but you must not let your family hear you say such things!'

'They'd probably applaud. They've been trying to get me married off for years. To save Richard the trouble, you know. I should warn you, before you accept, that I'm no great catch. I've a sharp tongue and a short temper. As a soldier's wife you'd be living in married quarters, wherever I may be posted.

You may have heard that I've money of my own; well, I have, and it takes time to look after it properly. Then I've no house to take you to. I inherited a small estate belonging to my mother's uncle, but the house there was burned down some twenty years ago and never rebuilt. When I finally leave the Army, I'll have to rent a place until I can build a house of my own. You mention my family; you know what I think of Richard, and the rest of them, with the exception of Agnes, are either disagreeable or foolish. I see as little of them as I can. My uncle Manning who lives in Town; he's well enough, and so are all his family. I think you'd like them.'

It was a long speech for a sick man. His voice failed. Frances closed her eyes. If only . . . Walter . . . false references. Richard . . . Gavin did not know . . . Her throat pained her. She put both her hands to it. She thought: "If only I could say 'yes'! If only he'd still been a younger son; if Walter had not ruined my chances of making a good marriage! I'd have made him a good wife, if things had been different! "

A door shut softly, nearby. Was it the door on to the Gallery? She had not been looking. She realised that if someone had peeped into the room, they would have thought his lordship asleep. He had not spoken for some time, and neither had she. He was lying still, watching her. She smoothed her hair and observed, in a commonplace voice, that Benson was taking his time.

'Benson approves,' said his lordship. '"There's a lady as would suit you to a T." That's what he said. Not that I needed him to point out the obvious to me. I have thought of very little except marrying you, from the moment I came to myself.'

Frances could not think of anything which she might safely say to that, so she busied herself around the room. When next Lord Broome opened his mouth to speak, she

104

stopped him, saying that he must conserve his energy, and try to sleep. He said he was not sleepy, but she noticed that he was lying almost flat on the bed, and that he looked exhausted. Within five minutes he was fast asleep.

Frances went out on to the Gallery and sent one of the maids for Polly. She was filled with nervous excitement. It was impossible for her to sit still, watching him, or she would begin to repeat the words of his proposal to herself, and build on them, and that would never do! Polly arrived to sit in the sick-room and Frances went upstairs to see the agency nurse. The woman had been very ill. She was lying in bed, shivering, her hair hanging around her face, and her skin pallid. She tried to get up when Frances came in, but her limbs would not support her. Frances felt sorry for her and asked if there were anything she might require. No, said the nurse; only something to calm her stomach. Perhaps the doctor would give her something when he arrived. Frances asked if the nurse knew what had made her ill. She did not. Perhaps her late-night cocoa, which had tasted strange. Perhaps it was just a chill.

Frances went downstairs to enquire if Dr Green had arrived yet, and was told that he'd come some time ago, and was closeted with Mr Broome and Mr Manning in the gun-room. This information was imparted by Spilkins, who seemed anxious to stand and gossip. He had heard, he said, that his lordship had

105

developed a fever. A slight one, said Miss Chard. It was a pity, Spilkins said, that his lordship had ever been taken off the quinine, for that would have prevented the fever.

'Quinine?' said Frances.

'The yellow stuff. Nurse Moon said she swore by it. It didn't taste too good, she said, but it worked a treat. A pity the bottle went astray when she left, for it might have saved his lordship's life.'

'Tasted nasty?' said Frances, beginning to suspect the truth.

'It certainly did. One of the footmen tried something his lordship had refused to eat, and he said it was enough to turn him off food for good. Young Abel, it was. A lad from a very low family. Serve him right, tasting food prepared for his betters. Well, I must get on. There's Mrs Broome fussing about her bracelet and it seems there's some money missing from the gun-room, too. I don't know what the world's coming to.' He held up a telegram form. 'I have to take this into the gun-room. Shall I tell the doctor you were enquiring for him?'

'The reply from the surgeon in London? At last!'

'From Bath. Not London. There hasn't been anything come from London, and it doesn't look as if the surgeon's coming, for it's long past time the train was due in.'

Bath. A telegram from Bath. But none

106

from London? It was a puzzle Frances could not solve. What did it mean? And why should there have been a telegram from Bath? Her aunt lived near Bath. Did it mean . . . could it mean that someone had telegraphed from the Court to her aunt? And if so, why? It could only be about Frances' references. Or was she reading too much into the situation? What ought she to do?

Unconsciously she wrung her hands. Theo . . . Lord Broome . . . the surgeon from London . . . the operation! She had given her promise to Lord Broome to see him through the operation, and she would do so, come what might.

Theo . . . what was he thinking of to delay like this? She started after Spilkins, only to be stopped by a cry from Polly, who came flying down the corridor after her.

'Oh, Miss—come quickly! It's the Reverend again, and he's brought the curate and candles and wants to set up an altar in the State Bedroom.'

'Whatever next!' cried Frances. She cast one longing glance down the corridor to the gun-room, and then hurried back along the Gallery, formulating plans to meet this unexpected attack.

*   *   *

To give him his due, Theo was suffering. He

knew that he was neglecting his patient, and he knew why, and he was beginning to feel that though no one else would blame him for causing Gavin's death by negligence, he himself would do so for the rest of his life. He forgot to puff at the cigar Hugo had given him, and his glass remained full at his side.

'A sad thing,' sighed Hugo. 'But of course his days were numbered, anyway. You say he would never have regained the use of the thumb and first finger on his left hand, whatever happened?'

'That's so,' said Theo. 'Of course, the damage was not done by the bullet which is causing all the trouble now. It was done way back in January, when his horse lashed out at him, breaking his arm and cutting through the tendons. A horse's hoof, slashing across an arm like that . . .' He shook his head. 'Very bad. He has not yet realised the truth. He thought power would return to the injured fingers when the splints were removed, and now he blames the bullet.' He lapsed into silence.

Mr Manning, sitting on the far side of the fireplace, was also miserable. He felt his presence at the Court was superfluous, because Hugo had so firmly taken over the reins of the household. He would every much have liked to return to his wife and children in London, but he could not in all decency leave while Gavin was dying.

'A hopeless case from the start,' said Hugo. 'You have handled it well, Doctor. If your uncle is no longer able to continue practising medicine, then be sure that the family will remember how well you have served them.'

Instead of pleasing Theo, this statement increased his feeling of guilt. 'Ought we not to telegraph again to London? It is strange that we have not even had an acknowledgment. What time was the telegram sent?'

'Arling took it to the telegraph office yesterday evening. My copy is here.' He held up a sheet of paper. 'It was sent at six yesterday.'

Theo had good sight, and moreover at that moment he had leaned forward to relight his cigar, so that the paper was well within his range. He started up, his cigar forgotten. 'It has been sent to the wrong man! I said Sir Stanley Ellis, not "Mr Trellis"! Oh, my God— what are we to do now?'

'The wrong . . .?' Hugo seemed as shaken as Theo. 'Are you sure? How could I have come to make such a mistake? I was sure . . . Uncle, do you remember exactly what it was that Doctor Green said?'

'I'm afraid not.' Mr Manning looked from one agitated young man to the other. 'What does it mean?'

'Such a mistake! I am mortified!' said Hugo.

'So many hours lost!' said Theo, throwing away his cigar. 'That is what it means. It reduces the chances of a successful operation to nil.'

'But you said there was no hope, anyway,' said Hugo. 'Be reasonable, Doctor. A tragic mistake has occurred, and whether I misheard you, or whether you gave me the wrong name in the heat of the moment is neither here nor there. What is done cannot be undone. Of course we wanted the best man to attend my cousin, but . . . let me fill your glass again . . . from what you have said the operation could only have hastened my cousin's end.'

While Theo stood irresolute, there came a knock on the door. The girl he loved and hoped to marry stood there. They were waiting for him, she said. He noticed that she was not looking as composed as usual, that her hair was not as smoothly arranged, and that her nostrils were flattened as if she were suppressing anger. He heard Hugo saying that they could not hope for a surgeon to arrive that day, and he heard her reply that she knew they had not yet received an answer from London.

'The telegram went to the wrong man,' said Theo. 'It was a mistake. I hardly know how it happened.'

She inclined her head, and he realised that she had noted his plea of not guilty, and refused to accept it. She stood aside from the door to allow him to pass before her, and sooner than lose her good opinion, he picked up his bag and went with her. She walked rapidly beside him along the corridor, her head bent and her fingers busy at the nape of her neck, smoothing her hair up into its coil. He touched her on the arm.

'I must speak to you.'

'What . . . now?' They were at the corner, by the turret stairs. She glanced round into the Gallery. 'You realise you must operate yourself, immediately?'

'I always meant to do so, if the surgeon did not arrive in time. You knew that?'

'I know that Lord Broome trusted you to do so.'

'And you? You know I would not have let him down?'

She preferred not to answer, but turned her head away from him.

'Miss Chard. Frances. I know that this is not the place, or the time to speak of marriage, but I have been half out of my mind since . . .'

'Marriage? You talk to me of marriage?' She spoke in a rapid monotone, unlike her usual manner of speech, and her eyes went now up the stairs, and now over his shoulder into the Gallery. 'I do not think of marriage. I do not think I shall ever marry. Come, they are waiting for us. I suggested that the vicar set up a chapel in Mrs Broome's ante-room. Benson is arranging everything in the Gallery. Lord Broome is—or was—asleep, but he keeps moving his arm about. He has a slight fever, I

111

think.'

'Why should you not marry me?'

'Hush, someone is coming.' Meakins, the ladies' maid, came down the turret stairs and passed them with eyes down, discretion written into every line of her body. No doubt she had heard what they had been saying, Theo thought. And no doubt Mrs Broome and Maud would hear of it within the hour. Frances was impatient.

'This is neither the time nor the place for such a discussion,' she said.

'But you promise me that you will think of it? You like me well enough, don't you?'

She looked him full in the eye. 'I liked you very well indeed,' she said, emphasising her use of the past tense.

'It was not I who made the mistake over the telegram.'

'Prove it by operating at once.'

Benson had improvised an operating table on one of the big chests in the Gallery, directly in the light of the windows. There were more servants in the Gallery than there should have been at that time of day. Housemaids were still busy making beds and turning out bedrooms, and there were no less than four footmen busying themselves with jobs which Frances had never seen done at that hour of the day before.

She went into the sick-room, leaving Theo to lay out the tools of his trade. Lord

112

Broome was restless, but asleep. She touched him on the hand and he woke, but not to full consciousness.

'I couldn't find her,' he said, looking straight up at her, but not seeing her. He was breathing with difficulty, as if he had been running. 'The weeds nearly got me, that time.' He frowned, blinked and turned his head to look round the room. 'Where . . .? Ah, I remember.' He looked at her, and this time he saw her. 'Did I say something stupid? I was having another of my nightmares. Is the surgeon here already?'

'We are going to carry you out into the Gallery, where the light is better. Theo will get the bullet out, and you will feel better then.'

'So soon?' Yes, he was afraid, and fighting for control. 'Give me something to hold on to. Something hard.'

She put the glass stopper into his hand. He grasped it firmly, and nodded to her to carry on. Two footmen carried the patient into the Gallery. Frances walked beside them, her eyes on Lord Broome's face. The removal from one place to another must have caused him pain, but he gave no sign of it.

Theo beckoned to her. 'They say the agency nurse is unfit, so you will have to assist me. Find yourself an apron, or you may soil your dress.'

'I know nothing of such things,' said Frances, eyeing the sharp blades on the table near by. When Theo tested the edge of a small

113

saw, she gasped, guessing it was intended for use during amputations.

'You will not faint?' said Theo.

'Of course she won't,' said Lord Broome, doing his best to smile at her.

'I'll try not to,' said Frances. Polly handed her an apron, and she put it on. Spilkins had appeared and was dispersing his staff about their normal duties, scolding as he did so. From the ante-room she could hear the rise and fall of the vicar's voice in prayer.

Theo hovered over his patient, rolling up the sleeve of his nightgown. 'I'd like to give you an anaesthetic. Miss Chard can administer it.'

'No,' said Lord Broome. 'I can stand pain, and I like to see what's going on.'

'Take the edge off it with brandy?' suggested Theo.

'No,' said Lord Broome. 'But have some yourself, by all means.' He grinned at Theo. 'I know just what you feel like. You'll be all right once you start.'

Theo rolled up his own shirt-sleeves, and pulled on an ancient apron, discoloured and encrusted with dried blood. Frances judged his nerves to be in a worse state than Lord Broome's. Theo's hands trembled as he positioned Lord Broome's arm. Lord Broome said something to Theo which she did not catch, but whatever it was, the young doctor laughed, and this seemed to steady him.

114

'No sense in hoping for a miracle,' he said, setting to work. 'No anaesthetic, no qualified assistance . . . badly bruised . . . badly cut . . . I can see where the bullet went in, but where is it now, eh?' He kneaded the arm, feeling for the bullet. Lord Broome, who had been lying with his head turned to the window and his eyes open, released his hold on the stopper. It fell off the improvised operating table and rolled between Frances' feet. She remarked in a small voice that she rather thought their patient had fainted.

'Just as well,' grunted Theo. 'This may be a long job. I think I can feel . . . yes, I'm sure I felt it just then . . . but getting it out without doing any further damage . . . the very devil is in it . . .'

Frances could feel the eyes of the servants on her. She felt useless, standing there, doing nothing. One footman and one maid had been left at each end of the Gallery to await orders and keep visitors out. In spite of the chill of the Gallery, Theo's face soon became red with exertion. Suddenly he began to fling orders at her. 'Hand me this . . . not that . . . the next one along . . .' Leaning over to hand Theo a knife, she caught a whiff of sweat and blood which caused vomit to rise in her throat. She fought it down, clinging to the chest. Theo shouted, 'Brandy!' She lifted her head to repeat his request, thinking that at all costs she must stay on her feet, and saw Benson heaving his guts out into a bowl nearby. Polly lifted her hand in token that she had understood, and vanished. 'Take it easy!' said Theo. Her hands trembled. She dropped a knife Theo passed to her, and it fell to the floor. Her hands were smeared with blood. The brandy arrived. At Theo's direction, Polly poured out a generous measure, and told Frances to drink it. After that, Frances' stomach obeyed her, and her hands obeyed Theo.

It seemed a long time before Theo drew a distorted bullet from Lord Broome's arm, and began the task of repair. Frances' fingers flew at the doctor's command. He commended her. When Lord Broome stirred back into consciousness, Frances put the stopper back into his right hand and told him that they had nearly finished. His eyes were glazed with pain, but he neither moaned nor cried out. Finally Theo sounded his patient's chest with his stethoscope, and stood back, motioning the footmen to carry Lord Broome back to bed. By that time both doctor and nurse were tired to the point of dropping. Their arms, their clothes and their faces were spattered with blood. Frances thought her dress was ruined, for she had not been able to afford good material, and it would shrink in the wash. Her mind dwelled alternately on the smile which Lord Broome had given her as he was borne away, and the fact that in his half-waking state that morning he had told her something of importance, that he had indeed dived into the water to rescue the drowning woman. "The weeds nearly got me, that time", he had said. Whom had he thought he was speaking to, in his re-creation of the fatal moments in which Lilien Jervis had drowned? In his nightmare he had been speaking to someone, that was certain. When he had given evidence, Lord Broome had implied that he had been alone when Lilien fell into the river, but Frances was now sure that he had had company on that occasion. But if so, why had the other person not spoken up to support the story which Major Broome had told at the inquest?

'Well, I've done what I can,' said Theo, as he removed his apron and began to put his knives away. 'If that wound becomes infected, he's likely to die, anyway. He must be watched, night and day. He mustn't be left alone, whatever happens. His heart and lungs are sound. With luck, he may pull through, but we don't want any more interference, do we? You do understand what I'm talking about?'

The servants were already clearing away the evidence of the operation under Spilkins's direction. The butler was agitated. The young ladies wished to return to their rooms . . . luncheon was going to be late . . . hurry, girl! Theo took her elbow and walked her to the far end of the Gallery, where there were no servants to overhear them.

'I'll be back this evening to have another

117

look at him. If he is going to pull through, he'll make a rapid recovery. But if the fever returns, or if . . . am I imagining things, Frances?'

She thought of monkish visitors and missing keys, and shook her head.

'I promise he'll be watched round the clock. Which reminds me; you ought to see the agency nurse before you go. She really has been very ill.'

'Yes. Do you think that her sickness . . .? No, it couldn't be the same, could it? Frances.' He hesitated. 'You don't object to my calling you Frances?'

'No, Theo. I don't object.'

His ugly face split in a grin. 'And you'll remember what we spoke of earlier? You will not forget?'

'I am not likely to forget anything that has happened this morning, but I am not likely to change my mind about marrying you, either.' She put her hand on his arm to soften her refusal, but her eyes were steady.

*   *   *

By the time Theo came to make his report to Hugo, he had begun to doubt his recollections of what he had actually said on the subject of sending for his old chief. Could he be absolutely sure that he had asked for the telegram to be sent to Sir Stanley Ellis? Had he perhaps mumbled the name, in his preoccupation with his own troubles?

Thus it was that the doctor answered the questions put to him by Hugo and Mr Manning somewhat at random. They put his abstraction down to worry about his patient, and assured Theo that they knew he had done his best.

After the doctor had gone, Hugo said to his uncle that he supposed the operation had been necessary, although personally he would have allowed the poor beggar to die in peace. Doctors were all alike, said Hugo. Never happy unless they were cutting you up.

'A more important question,' said Mr Manning, 'is what we are to do about Miss Chard. Her aunt's telegram made it clear that she lied to Mrs Broome about the length of time she was teaching in Bath. Shall you telegraph this woman, Mrs Palfrey, for details?'

'Yes, I think I must. There may be nothing in it, but we cannot be too careful when the education of the young is at stake.'

'Young Doctor Green seems to think highly of her. By the way, if that new Will hasn't been sent off to the solicitors yet, I'd be glad of another look at it.'

Hugo's hand went to a certain drawer in the bureau while his fingers sought for the key on his key-ring. The drawer, which ought to have been locked, opened under his hand. He rose from his chair, and looked inside the drawer. 'It's not there,' he said. And then, 'But it must be! You saw me put the Will in there, didn't you? And I'm sure I locked the drawer, afterwards.'

He ransacked the bureau, but the Will, like the money which had been left there by Richard, had disappeared. The bell was rung and Spilkins, who had been on the point of announcing luncheon, was cross-questioned instead about visitors to the gun-room. Spilkins declared that he knew nothing about the new Will, and neither—or so they said—did any of the servants when they were questioned by Hugo. What did emerge from the enquiry was that a spare key to the bureau was usually kept in a tobacco jar on the mantelpiece in the gun-room, and that everyone knew of it. It had been put there because Master Richard had once lost the key to the bureau, with all his papers locked up inside it. As to visitors to the gun-room, it was impossible to tell. The servants would pass its door a dozen times a day on their way to the Great Hall and the dining-room. As for the family, Spilkins could not—or would not—be drawn.

'Quite right,' said Mr Manning to Hugo, in an undertone. 'We cannot ask the servants to inform on their employers. We must ask the family ourselves.'

The Broome family were waiting in the Great Hall for lunch to be announced. The

vicar and his curate had suspended their
prayers to join them. Mr Manning broke the
news to them of the Will's disappearance,
while Hugo chewed on an unlit cigar. Mrs
Broome cried out, and reached for her salts.
Lady Amelia's jaw dropped, and she blinked.
Isabella wondered aloud if she would be
restored to her previous position as heiress.

Maud sprang to her feet and stared at
Hugo. She wanted to know if he intended this
development to make any difference to his
conduct towards her. Was she as desirable to
him without her inheritance? Hugo seemed
unable to answer. For the first time since
his arrival at the Court, he was less than
composed. Whether or no he intended to
repulse her, Maud evidently thought that he
did. She closed her eyes, opened her mouth
and screamed. Such a breach of good manners
was bad, but what followed was worse. Her
skirts swinging, Maud leaped upon Isabella
and, seizing her by the shoulders, began to
shake her.

'You! You stole it!' she panted. 'You
thieving snake! You . . .!' She pulled Isabella
out of her seat. 'Give it back!'

A red mark appeared on Isabella's cheek
and her hair tumbled down as Maud slapped
her. Isabella began to weep. She begged Maud
to let her go. Maud did not hear her. Twining
her fingers in her cousin's curls, Maud threw
Isabella to the floor and began to beat her

head against the floor. All was uproar. The vicar was calling upon Maud to desist, Mr Manning was trying to seize one of Maud's hands.

'I'll tear it out of you! Tell me where you put it! You . . .'

It took the combined efforts of Mr Manning, the vicar and the curate to pull Maud off Isabella, and by that time the poor girl was a shivering wreck of her former self. As soon as she found herself physically restrained, Maud commanded herself sufficiently to stand still.

'Send for the police,' she said. 'Search her room. Look in the writing desk that she uses. Strip her bed. Strip her. Maybe she's got it on her at the moment.'

'Oh, Maud!' cried Mrs Broome, in tears. 'How could you!'

Isabella hobbled to her godmother, and sank in tears at her feet. Lady Amelia, white-faced, helped the trembling girl to her feet and announced that if someone would be so kind as to summon their maid, she thought they had better retire to their rooms. They would naturally be leaving the Court as soon as their things had been packed. Mr Manning made as if to help Lady Amelia, who was trembling almost as much as her granddaughter, but the old lady refused his assistance as she led Isabella from the room.

'I shall go for the police myself if you

don't send for them,' said Maud. 'I do not intend to be defrauded of my rights by that— that whey-faced chit. If none of you are men enough to protect me, I must take steps to protect myself.' And here she looked at Hugo, who had taken no part in the scuffle, but was standing in his usual place on the hearth-rug.

'No police,' said Mr Manning. 'We can settle this without a scandal. I think I can persuade Amelia to stay, and to agree that a search is made of their rooms, provided that we also agree to a search being made of our own rooms. You may start with mine, if you wish. Hugo . . .?'

'Yes,' said Hugo heavily. 'That's a good idea. If only it hasn't been destroyed already. I can see no other reason why it should have been taken.'

'If you please, sir,' said Spilkins. He had been an interested but unnoticed spectator of the scene. 'Would this solve your problem?' He proffered a silver salver on which lay a folded sheet of paper. 'I found this note in the pocket of my coat just now. Someone must have put it there while it was hanging on its peg in the pantry. Or perhaps it's been there since last night. I didn't look in the pocket until just now, when I wanted a pencil. It seems to explain everything.'

Hugo took the note and read it to himself. He exclaimed, 'Gracious Heavens!'

He held up his hand to attract everyone's

attention. 'Listen to this, everyone. I'll read it out to you. "Are you so stupid that you can't see what's under your nose? Benson is carrying the stolen gold on him, in a body belt. Nothing went wrong till he arrived, and he's been at the bottom of everything that's gone wrong since. Can't you see that he made up that story about two men getting into the carriage at Lewes? Can't you see that it was he who attacked and robbed his master?" There's no date on it, and it's signed "A Friend".'

CHAPTER FIVE

The idea of searching the Court was abandoned. A message was sent up by two of the footmen to the sick-room, to ask Benson to present himself forthwith in the Great Hall. Frances was not there; worn out, she had given Polly her stained dress and lain down on her bed to sleep. The agency nurse was not there; although recovering, she was still in her room. Lord Broome was fast asleep; he had not moved since he was laid back in his bed, and he was so deeply asleep that he did not even hear the altercation over his head.

'I don't care what Mr Hugo wants me for,' said Benson. 'I'm not leaving the Major alone.'

One of the footmen volunteered to take a turn at the bedside. Benson scrutinised him from head to toe, and demanded to know his name. It was Abel, the lad who had been suspected of dressing up as a monk the other night. Benson hummed and hawed and said all right, he supposed Abel would do for a while, and that if the Major stirred, someone must go for Miss Chard at once.

In the Great Hall the family were still waiting for their luncheon. Lady Amelia and Isabella had been called back to witness the confrontation with Benson, and a good many of the servants had managed to crowd into the doorway to hear and see what they could.

Mr Manning read the anonymous note out to Benson, and asked if he had anything to say.

'No,' said Benson, more annoyed at being taken from his post than afraid. 'Except it's obviously a load of nonsense. What would I want to harm the Major for?'

'For the legacy he'd left you in his first Will. When you found out he'd made another Will you were very upset, weren't you?'

'Well, I did wonder what was going on. It wasn't like him to change his mind without telling me.'

'So you stole the second Will from the bureau, as you'd previously stolen your master's money, and the money Lord Richard had left there.'

'What the blazes . . .?' demanded Benson.

'If you are innocent, you won't object to being searched, will you?'

'Stop!' cried Benson, as hands were laid on him. 'Of course I've got his money on me. I don't mind showing you, if you keep your hands off!'

'You admit it, then?'

'He gave it me to carry for him when we landed . . .'

'A likely tale!'

Benson pulled up his shirt and took off a body belt that was girt around him. In silence, Hugo Broome took the belt off the batman, and counted out twenty-seven gold sovereigns from the belt on to the table.

'Where is Mrs Broome's bracelet?' he asked. 'And the rest of the money you stole from the gun-room? This is only part of it. And where is the missing Will? Have you destroyed it already? Confess, or it will be the worse for you.'

'I have nothing to confess. And give that money back. It's not yours, it's the Major's.'

'We are very well aware of that. All right,' to the footmen. 'Take him away. Lock him up in some secure place—one of the store-rooms in the old part of the house will do. And send Arling to fetch the police from Lewes.'

Only then did Benson realise the danger of his position. He did not go quietly when they laid hands on him, and his shouts and the sound of the blows he gave and received echoed round the Great Hall. Unfortunately for him, the Court was solidly built, and the

126

noise did not penetrate to the schoolroom, or to the State Bedroom. Those who might have defended him were sound asleep.

Over lunch, Hugo summed up the position.

'So, now we have the evidence to prove that Benson attacked his master, and that he made up that story about two men entering the compartment at Lewes. I must say it is a relief to have that business cleared up. But we don't have my aunt's bracelet, the balance of the money from the gun-room, or the missing Will.'

'Meakins told me that Benson has been seen playing cards in the village with a bad type of man. Perhaps he's lost the rest of Richard's money, gambling. And maybe Mama's bracelet went the same way.'

'And he would have destroyed the second Will,' said Mr Manning. 'Knowing that it cut him out of any share of Gavin's money. I wonder what he did to cause Gavin to disinherit him. Perhaps if Gavin had learned that his batman was addicted to gambling . . .?'

'What about the Will?' Maud asked the question which was in all their minds. 'Does Isabella inherit? Doesn't the fact that we all know there was a second Will and can testify to it in court, mean that the second Will should stand?'

Mr Manning signed for the servants to leave the room. 'I think,' he said, 'that we should have a family conference on the matter. I do not think any of us would wish to go to law about it. Perhaps some adjustment within the framework of Gavin's known intentions . . .?'

'You mean that I have to give Isabella a portion of the money, to keep her quiet? Well, I won't, and that's flat.'

'Maud, dear,' said Mrs Broome nervously. 'Perhaps I could have a word with you in private . . .'

'That money is rightfully mine,' said Isabella. 'If Maud had been nice to me about it, I might have considered giving her some few hundred pounds, but considering the way she has treated me . . .'

'Isabella,' said Lady Amelia. 'There is much in what your uncle says. You could easily spare two hundred a year, say . . .'

'Two hundred!'

Everyone began to talk at once.

*   *   *

Frances woke in the early twilight. She had only one other day dress, also grey, also home-made. As she put it on she suppressed a sigh. Isabella and Maud both talked of poverty, but Frances would have given a great deal for one of their cast-off dresses at that moment. To have been able to appear before Lord Broome in one of Maud's trousseau dresses, for instance; there was one of pale yellow velvet with a pleated underskirt which would have

128

suited Frances better than it suited the person for whom it had been made.

The house seemed unearthly quiet as she made her way down to the sick-room. She was not to know that at that very minute practically all the servants in the house were watching as Benson was hauled into a closed cab by two large policemen sent out from Lewes to arrest him for attempted murder and robbery. Abel, the footman, was sitting outside the sickroom door; he sprang to his feet when he saw her. He did not realise that she knew nothing of Benson's arrest. He told her that he was taking the afternoon watch for Benson, but that his lordship had told him to wait outside the door. She accepted his explanation without thinking anything of it.

Lord Broome was sitting upright, away from the pillows. He had taken his left arm from the sling which Theo had contrived for him, and his crippled hand lay hidden under the bedclothes. He looked very much alive, and as if he were in pain.

'Your arm is hurting you?' she asked, aware of the dangers of infection.

'I'm done for,' he said.

She did not understand. She touched his forehead and judged the fever to have left him.

'Did you know all along?' he asked. 'Why didn't you tell me? No, that's not fair. I knew, myself. Right from the beginning. But I didn't want to admit it.'

'You're not to talk like that. You're not going to die. You are the type who lives to be eighty and damns the younger generation and tells everyone the world is going to the dogs.'

He smiled, briefly. 'Just like my grandfather. No, I wasn't talking about dying, but about my hand. It's no good, is it? Taking the bullet out hasn't made any difference to my thumb and forefinger. I'm crippled.' He repeated the words to himself, silently, as if trying to get used to the idea. 'I made you an offer of marriage on the understanding that I'd come through the operation all right. Well, I release you from that. You won't want a one-handed man. Who would? The Army won't, either. I've been trying to think what the devil I'm going to do with the rest of my life. I've never thought of being anything but a soldier since I was twelve, and now . . . Politics are out, at least until people have forgotten what happened last year. I've done for myself there. I didn't realise at the time . . . Perhaps I'll go on a world tour. I've always wanted to go to Greece. But what would I do when I got there? I've no taste for an idle life.'

Frances stopped trying to pretend that she was a disinterested nurse. She took his injured hand out from under the bedclothes and tried to rub life into the thumb and forefinger. They remained limp and unresponsive.

'You see?' He smiled, without mirth. 'Dead as my career.

I told myself that when the splints were removed . . . when the bullet was taken out . . . but I knew all along. I've seen injuries like this before.'

'I don't see that it matters that much. It's only your left hand.'

'Theo didn't tell you? I'm left-handed. I can't write, or do anything properly with my right hand. I know, because I tried as a child.'

She cried out, and put the maimed hand to her cheek.

'Some women have no sense at all,' said his lordship. 'Didn't you hear me say that my offer of marriage is withdrawn?'

'I couldn't accept it, anyway.'

'Why not?'

She tried to make a joke of it. She took herself over to the window and looked out. 'Oh, because you'd always want the last word in an argument. What woman would stand for that?'

He laughed, this time genuinely amused. 'There's that,' he admitted. 'But then, I don't want a woman who is incapable of forming an opinion of her own. I want someone who is prepared to stand up to me, and tell me if she thinks I'm overstepping the mark. A companion, as well as a wife.'

She thought: This is dreadful; he really cares for me. I must stop him, before he goes any further. If only . . .

'Is it because of what happened last

131

summer?' he asked. 'I give you my word that I did not drown that girl.'

'Oh, I believe you.'

'You do? No one else does.'

'The more fools they.'

'Agreed. Then, if it is not that . . .? Ah, I've got it. You want me to make you long flowery speeches on my knees, about how beautiful you are, and how I'd go to the ends of the earth to fetch you a rare flower and all that rot. Well, it may be the accepted method of proposing for a young, romantic idiot, but I'm neither young nor romantic and I'm hanged if I'll go down on my knees to any woman, even you. Even if I could manage it without falling flat on my face.'

She had to laugh. 'It isn't that. But you can't really expect me to take you seriously. Miss Seld treated you badly, you are temporarily at a standstill, perhaps you feel some gratitude towards me for nursing you. In a few days' time, when you are feeling better, you will be ashamed of what you have said to me. So let us say no more about it. Think instead of what you can do on the estate when the weather improves; it is a beautiful place, but much neglected, as you must know. The tenants complain that repairs are never done, and the Court itself needs modernising. Could you not concern yourself with these matters in the immediate future?'

'And live. in my brother's shadow? No,

132

thank you. Granted, he would be delighted if I did. While I'm around, he doesn't have to trouble his head with business or money matters. Don't misunderstand me, I'm very fond of Richard, as he is of me, but I'll not live here as his agent. No, I think I'll go abroad. Doesn't the idea of a cruise in the Grecian Islands appeal to you?'

For a moment she was tempted. Why shouldn't she accept him? She would make him a good wife. She could be the sort of wife he wanted. And as for what the world might think . . .? She drew back.

'You know nothing about me, or you wouldn't make me a proposal of marriage. I was dismissed from my last place without a character, and heaven only knows how long Mrs Broome will keep me on, once she realises . . . Let us talk of something else. Shall I fetch a newspaper and read it to you?'

'So your last employer's husband tried to kiss you?'

'Much worse than that,' she said, with grim gaiety. 'I was accused of stealing, or rather, of putting a young man up to steal from his aunt, and of trying to trap him into marriage. The police were called in. I assure you that I am the wickedest creature alive; depraved, corrupt, unworthy to cross the threshold of a decent household. You see what I mean?'

'That's almost as bad as what they said about me,' said his lordship. He seemed

133

to be amused, rather than alarmed, by her disclosures. He patted the bed beside him, and leaned back on his pillows. 'Sit down and tell me all about it.'

'Will you, in turn, tell me all about Lilien Jervis?'

'Not at the moment. But I promise that one day I will tell you everything. Now, talk!'

'Well, about a year ago I went as governess to a Mrs Palfrey, of Gloucestershire. She had two small children; darlings, both of them. She treated me well, and encouraged me to join her in the drawing-room when there was company. Her husband was in India, and she had no relatives near, but about a mile away an old friend of hers lived, who was not strong and rarely left her own house. This lady— Mrs Donne—was very rich, and quite alone in the world except for her nephew, Walter. Mrs Palfrey was very fond of Mrs Donne, and we often took the children to Mrs Donne's for afternoon tea, or Mrs Palfrey would send me over with a book or a basket of fruit to Mrs Donne's. Walter was not always there. He was employed as a clerk by a distant relative in the City, but he did not like the work. He used to visit his aunt at weekends. Then, in June last year, he suggested to Mrs Donne that she make him an allowance so that he could give up his job and devote all his time to her. She agreed. I was flattered. I knew . . . he told me . . . that he had done this thing so that he could see more of me. He was young and good company, and at the time I thought him everything a gentleman should be. I admired him for his devotion to his aunt. I believed him when he said that he wished, one day, when his aunt could be brought round to the idea, that he wished, in short, to marry me. It was very foolish of me to listen to him, but he was the first person from my father's world . . . from the world in which I thought I had a right to move . . . to wish to marry me. I did encourage him to hope. I thought I loved him enough to wait for him, but . . . then he wanted me to run away with him. I was terribly upset. I could not understand why he wanted to be so precipitate. He had only to wait. Mrs Donne was very fond of me at that time, and my family background was not at all despicable. My father was a Colonel in the Army, and his family have lived on their estate near Taunton for six generations. It would not have been too unequal a match. Besides, I could not run away and leave Mrs Palfrey and my two darling little boys without notice.

'He apologised for upsetting me. He said a great many things about my having driven him to distraction and . . . well, you know the sort of things men say. He gave me a piece of jewellery and asked me to wear it, as a token that I forgave him his foolishness. I wore it, without attempting to conceal it. Why should I? I had no idea . . . But one day Mrs Donne came with Walter to call on us. It was the first time she had been out of her house for months. She saw the pendant and claimed it as hers. She had been missing pieces of jewellery over a period of some months. A maid had fallen under suspicion and been dismissed, but it was he—Walter—who had been taking her things all along. He had been gambling and got into debt. He'd stolen something of hers, and the theft had gone undetected, and he'd gone on stealing and grown careless enough to give me something he'd stolen.

'I couldn't believe it at first. I kept saying that there must be some mistake. The police came. Mrs Donne could not believe that Walter would have stolen from her on his own initiative. I told her everything, of course. I had notes from him to prove that he wanted to marry me. She was furious; she said she had plans to marry him to a god-daughter of hers who had a large fortune. She said some very hard things to me; that I had seduced Walter, and trapped him into . . . Oh, it was dreadful. At first I was indignant. But Walter, when he came face to face with me, he acted in such a weak manner, he could not look me in the eye . . . I could not believe that this was the same man who all summer had been urging me to . . .

'His aunt said that I had been to blame for everything. She forgave Walter, and said she would not bring charges against him provided

136

I left the district at once and did not attempt to communicate with him ever again. I did not wish to see him again after that, but I did not want to be thrown out of the house like that. The two little boys cried when they heard I was to go. Mrs Palfrey cried, too. She believed my story, but nevertheless she refused me a reference because Mrs Donne was such a very old friend of hers and influential, and, after all, I was only a governess, a nobody. So I went back to my aunt's school in Bath, and started writing around for another job. I lied to Mrs Broome and to your brother, saying that I had been at my aunt's all last summer and autumn. They will find out some day, of course.'

*   *   *

'Undoubtedly. You must get in first with your side of the tale. Benson and Polly tell me you are highly regarded by my aunt, and are considered to have worked wonders with that brat Agnes. My aunt won't want to lose you. I believe she even boasts to guests that you are of gentle birth. Are you related to the Chards of Somerset? I know a Rupert Chard slightly.'

'My cousin. He has six sisters, one about my age and the rest younger. They all have to be married off somehow. My father's family quarrelled with him when he married my mother because she was only a teacher and had no dowry. My mother's sister brought me up after my father and mother died. My aunt wrote to my uncle Chard when I was eighteen, hoping that he would do something for me. He and my aunt Chard visited us in Bath. They brought two of their daughters, my cousins, with them. I quite understood, after that, why they could do nothing for me.'

His lordship frowned. 'Bella and Ruth Chard? I think I've met them, too, at dances in Town. Both as plain as flat biscuits. No wonder your uncle and aunt didn't want you in the house, with that lot to marry off.'

She thought how marvellous it would have been to have had a Season in Town herself, and to have danced with Lord Broome on equal terms.

He had hidden his maimed hand under the coverlet again. She thought that he ought not to hide it away, or it would become an obsession with him.

'You mustn't let them get you down,' said his lordship. 'Hold your head high and tell them to go to blazes if they criticise you. I'll tell Richard for you, if you like. He won't hold it against you, if I put it to him the right way. And my aunt won't be able to say anything after that, because it's Richard who pays your salary. Right?'

She pulled his left hand from under the coverlet and warmed it between her hands. 'Your aunt will not understand. I hoped she would. I thought that when I'd been here a little while, and had established myself, I could tell her. But she is too . . .'

'Narrow-minded? I agree. I'll tell Richard first, and then you can "confess' to my aunt, and that way you'll be all right. I wish you'd leave my hand alone. Doesn't it revolt you?'

'Of course not.' She reached for the nail scissors and started to cut his nails. 'Don't hide it away. It only draws attention to it. If you ignore it, so will everyone else. Wear a glove on it, if you must, but don't allow a small thing like this to ruin your life.'

*   *   *

Theo heard the story of Benson's guilt while he was out on his rounds; like everyone else, he was at first surprised, and then chided himself for not having seen the obvious before. He visited Mrs Broome and the nurse before he went to the State Bedroom. Both had been confined to their rooms that afternoon. Mrs Broome wept as she told the doctor she was sure that Benson had sold her bracelet to cover his gambling debts, and that she would never see it again. Theo left her a soothing draught, and because he had made what was for him an enormous effort to appear interested in her palpitations, she was kind enough to say that in time he might become as good a doctor as his uncle.

This was pleasing to Theo. Moreover,

when he reached the sick-room he found Lord Broome not only conscious, but happily engaged in teasing his nurse. He was bright-eyed, but he had no fever, and the remains of his supper tray showed that he had dined well. The fire burned brightly, the lamp cast a mellow light, and altogether it was a scene which ought to have delighted a doctor. But Theo, after one professional glance which assured him that all was well with his patient, had eyes for no one but Frances, and it was plain that she had eyes for no one but Lord Broome. Perhaps she did not mean her hands to caress him as she tucked him in for the night; nevertheless Theo noted that they did in fact do so. He also noted that Lord Broome was making free of Miss Chard's first name, and that she did not appear to object.

'Tomorrow I shall sit in the chair for a while,' said Lord Broome. 'Frances doesn't think I shall be well enough, but then, she doesn't know anything about nursing. And I am to teach her how to play chess. I am quite shocked to learn that she does not know how to play. How is she to teach Agnes, if she can't play herself?'

'I would have been very willing to teach her myself, if I had known,' said Theo, acid in his voice.

'And I am to have a newspaper to read. I remember they signed a truce after I left South Africa, but . . .' He frowned, uncertain of his

140

memory. 'Benson got me a paper on Lewes station, and I was reading it when . . . What happened? You say two men attacked me?'

'Your memory is gradually returning. Don't try to force it.'

His lordship put his hand to his head. 'Where's Benson? Sloped off to the village?'

Theo looked at Frances, who returned his glance with one of enquiry. So she did not know about Benson, either? 'He's not well,' said the doctor.

'Has he been sick, too?' cried Frances. 'It's quite an epidemic. First the nurse, and now . . .'

'Sick?' repeated his lordship. 'Now what do I remember about that? A nurse. Not this present one, but another one. A bigger woman, who smelled of . . . The devil! My head aches.'

The doctor repeated his injunction against forcing things, measured out a sleeping draught and saw that Lord Broome drank it. Polly came in to remove the supper tray, and the agency nurse appeared. She looked pale but said she would be able to manage the night watch. Frances half drew the bedcurtain so that the lamp should not shine on the sick man's face, and followed the doctor out into the Gallery.

Theo caught Frances by the arm, and drew her away from the sick-room door. The Gallery was deserted; the family were all in the music-room, and the servants shunned this part of the house at night. Rain beat against the windows. In a few words, Theo told Frances about Benson. At first she could not believe that he was serious. Even when she was convinced that Benson had been arrested, she still refused to believe in his guilt.

'We must ask Lord Broome about the money which was found on Benson. I am sure Benson said something . . . or Lord Broome did . . . about Benson looking after money for him. I am sure Benson is innocent.'

'We must not wake him. He must be asleep by now. If what you say is true, then we must wait till the morning, and go into the matter properly. We can't get him out of Lewes jail tonight, whatever we do. Be sensible.'

Reluctantly, she agreed to wait.

'Another thing,' said Theo. 'I don't quite know how to put this, but Gavin may possibly try to flirt with you to while away the time that he is laid up. A trained nurse would of course recognise his advances for what they were worth.'

'That idea had already occurred to me,' said Frances, her colour rising. 'I don't mind, if it will help him through a bad time. His hand— why didn't you tell me he was left-handed? Can nothing be done?'

'You think another doctor might have done better? The damage was done back in January.'

'I am sorry. Of course, you did all you could. But I feel so sorry for him. He still has to be told of his brother's death. He talks of him all the time, as if he were aware, subconsciously, that something is wrong. He watches me, when he mentions his brother, as if to catch me out . . . She put up a finger to flick at the corner of her eye. 'He is a born fighter, as you said. He will come through.'

'So long as you realise he is using you.'

Frances said it was very cold in the Gallery, and that if there was nothing else, she proposed to go to bed. Theo watched her out of sight. It was only that morning that he had realised he loved her. There was so much that he would have liked to say to her, but it seemed as if the time when he might have said it was already in the past.

*   *   *

The fire had been allowed to go out in the schoolroom, and there was none in either of the nurseries since Agnes and Nurse had gone. Frances wondered if this was an oversight on the part of the servants, or whether it was an extension of the treatment which had first been meted out to Lord Broome. Was her welfare to be neglected because she was his nurse?

She was tired, in spite of her nap that afternoon, so she decided against ringing for

143

someone to make up the fire. She would go straight to bed. Someone—probably Polly—had left a plate of bread and butter and a glass of barley water on the table for her. She ate the bread and butter while she undressed and brushed out her hair. Then she picked up the barley water. Fatigue made her reactions slow. She had swallowed two mouthfuls before she realised that anything was wrong, and it was only after she had been hanging over her basin, retching, for what seemed like hours that her mind began to work again.

She did not know how long it was before she could force her shaking limbs to carry her to the stairs. She staggered down them, holding on to the rail. The lamps had been removed from the Gallery, and she had to feel her way along it in the dark. Everyone must be in bed. It must be very late. There was a foul taste in her mouth. A burning taste; the same taste which had been present in the food and drink which Lord Broome had refused, and which might have caused the agency nurse's inconvenient sickness that day.

Suppose that the nurse had been made ill in order to keep her away from the operating table, and thus reduce the chance of Lord Broome's survival? Suppose that she herself had been given another dose, in order to keep her quietly in her own room . . . suppose that the nurse was asleep, as she might well be after having been ill all day . . . and Benson out of the way . . . Lord Broome unprotected . . . in a room which could not be secured against intruders without Benson's assistance . . .

The sick-room door was closed, but a gaping shadow further along the Gallery showed that the door to the dressing-room, which had for so long been locked, was now ajar. Frances pushed it open, and entered. The room was dimly lit by a night-light; the agency nurse lay on the cot, and to judge by her heavy breathing she was fast asleep. Frances shook her arm, but the woman did not stir.

The communicating door to the sick-room was open, and a glow showed that a lamp still burned within. As it should do. Frances listened, and heard nothing but the breathing of the nurse at her side. Perhaps she had been mistaken in thinking his lordship in danger. How absurd she must look, running around the house in the middle of the night, barefooted, in her night-gown, with her hair hanging down her back!

Was that a noise? A rustle? A groan?

She lunged for the communicating door, pushed it open, and screamed.

A shadow reached across the counterpane of the bed towards her; it was the cowled monk, who stood between her and the lamp. He was on the far side of the bed, holding something above the head of the sick man. He turned his head towards Frances, but his face was in shadow, so that she could not make out

145

his features. She screamed again. The cowled figure shrank and disappeared behind the bed-curtains. By the time she had rounded the bed Lord Broome was sitting up, and the door to the Gallery was swinging shut behind the intruder. She fell over something on the floor, and was brought to her knees. It was a pillow. The pillow which had been held above Lord Broome's head, as he lay helpless on the bed. In falling, Frances struck her head against the side of the bed, and the room tilted around her.

Her memory of the next few minutes was confused. By the time the room had righted itself, she was sitting on the bed with his lordship's sound arm round her, being very thoroughly kissed. Instead of repulsing him as she ought to have done, she tightened her clutch on his nightshirt. She was tired and frightened and she still felt sick, so very naturally she began to cry.

She did not know what to do, or to whom she could turn for advice. She was now sure that Benson had been right in his suspicions of Nurse Moon, and she was equally sure that she herself had just frustrated another attempt on Lord Broome's life, but he did not know this, and she did not know how to tell him or, even more important, how to keep him safe from further harm. She had a clear recollection of having screamed when she had seen the monk, and yet nobody had come to her aid. True, these old walls were thick, but . . . who slept next door? Old Lady Amelia? Maud?

To add to her problems, it appeared that Lord Broome, instead of being frightened, was enjoying himself. Frances found herself being kissed in places and in ways that Walter had never . . . she had never dreamed . . . it was absurd . . . she could not be so abandoned as to enjoy . . . ?

Some minutes later Lord Broome ordered her to stay where she was, got himself off the bed and promptly collapsed on to the floor. He was furious with himself, but his weakness brought Frances to her senses as nothing else could have done. She got him back on to the bed and then obeyed his instructions to fetch a battered wooden writing desk that stood on top of a cupboard nearby. Opening it, Lord Broome extracted a flask, and poured out a tot of whisky for her. 'One of Richard's little secrets,' he said. 'He's not much of a penman, and it amuses him to keep spirits where the ink should be. Now drink up, and calm down. That was no ghost, if that is what you were thinking. Just a man dressed up in a robe to frighten me.'

'You know who it was?' gasped Frances, who was not used to strong drink. Twice in one day . . .! What would her aunt have said?

'I think it was probably Lee, although I did not see his face. No one else has that build, and a grudge against me.'

'But—who is Lee?'

'He is, or was, rather, Lilien's father. Now I know what you are going to ask. If I didn't kill her, why should he want to kill me? Well, I didn't, and he knows that I didn't, but he's not sure who was responsible for Lilien's pregnancy, and as it was that which was indirectly responsible for her death . . .' He shrugged. 'Why, you are trembling!' He had his arm round her, so he ought to know. 'My darling, much as I appreciate your appearance at my bedside in your nightgown, I cannot help thinking that others might place a construction on your behaviour which . . .'

'Oh!' cried Frances, and started to cry again. Weeping, she blurted out not only the story of the attempt to poison her, but also the news of Benson's arrest and removal to Lewes jail. His lordship heard her out in silence, renewed the whisky in her cup, and observed that it seemed to be about time he was up and about again. 'And what else are you hiding from me?'

'N-nothing. I mean, nothing much. What I mean is, were you responsible for that girl's pregnancy?'

He kissed her. 'Would you mind if I were?'

'I ought to,' confessed Frances, her moral fibre weakened by the whisky and proximity to his lordship. 'Only, somehow it really doesn't seem to be very important whether you were or not.'

'My dear girl!' said his lordship, scandalised.

148

'Don't let my aunt hear you!'

'It must be the whisky.' Frances giggled. 'You weren't responsible?'

'No, I wasn't.' He kissed the tip of her nose. 'I might have been, but I wasn't. Now, off to bed with you before I'm responsible for something else. Rouse the nurse and get her to understand that she's got to put a chair under the knob of both doors as soon as you've gone. And don't wake anyone else up on your way back to your own room. I don't want my future wife falling foul of Maud's tongue.'

'I am not going to marry you,' said Frances, rising to her feet with enormous dignity.

'Come back here,' said his lordship, 'and we'll talk it over.'

Frances fled.

*   *   *

Perhaps because of the whisky, Frances slept well, and the only reminder of her night's ordeal was a slight shakiness in her limbs as she dressed next morning. As she went down the stairs she resolved to ask for an interview with Mrs Broome as soon as possible. Of course, she must confess her past history to Mrs Broome, but more important than that, she must also tell her about the attempts on Lord Broome's life. It was not sensible to keep such matters secret. The police must be informed; it would not be necessary to mention the fact that she had been dressed only in a night-gown when she went into the sick-room last night.

And then there was the matter of Benson; she was sure he was innocent, but she was not so sure that Mrs Broome would be capable of getting him out of Lewes jail. It might perhaps be advisable to ask for an interview with Mr Manning on the subject. Mr Manning struck Frances as being a sensible, honest man, and if she could only convince him of Benson's innocence, he would be a valuable ally and perfectly capable of dealing with the police. It was significant that she never once thought of applying to Hugo for aid.

And then she must break the news to Lord Broome of his brother's death. This she planned to do gently; perhaps on the following day. Lord Broome thought he would be fit to get out of bed that day. She thought he wanted to do too much too quickly. He did not realise how ill he had been.

All her plans went awry. When she reached the sick-room, Lord Broome was already sitting up in bed, her shawl over his dressing-gown, and Abel was shaving him. Lord Broome had a sling round his neck, but his hand was more often out of it than in, and by the look of his breakfast tray he had eaten more than Frances. He greeted her with the information that the agency nurse was a fool, and that he'd packed her off out of the way.

'If you please, Major!' cried Abel, brandishing his razor. All the servants had been warned to address Lord Broome as "Major".

'Hurry!' said Lord Broome. 'I've got to get Benson out of jail, and I suppose I'll have to see the family, too. My aunt and godmother will cry, and my cousins stay the minimum amount of time and wish themselves elsewhere. Frances, fetch me some clothes. Not one of my uniforms; they'll be no use to me in the future.' He was in high spirits.

The door opened to reveal Meakins, the ladies' maid.

'If you please, Miss,' she said, addressing Frances, 'The Reverend has arrived and is wishful to see his lordship. Also Mrs Broome wants to know when the doctor is coming up to see his lordship. She's had another of her bad turns.'

For a moment no one either moved or spoke. The smile on Frances' face froze. Everyone, but every single person at the Court knew that Gavin Broome was unaware of his brother's death, and that he must be guarded from such knowledge until he was better. How dared this woman break the embargo?

'Later,' said Frances. 'I will see you later.' She seized Meakins by the elbow and whirled her out into the Gallery. And shut the door on her. One look at his lordship's face taught her that the damage was done. A man less quickwitted might not have noticed anything, but Gavin Broome had.

'What was that she said?' he asked. He signed Abel to complete his task. The footman's face . . . Frances firmed her shoulders against the wood of the door and took a deep breath.

'Thank goodness the rain has stopped,' she said. 'The daffodils in the park must have been beaten flat these last few days, and heaven only knows if there will be enough left to decorate the altar in church this Sunday. Easter, you know.'

Abel finished shaving his master, gathered his things together, and left.

'Did she think Richard was here?' he asked. 'No, how could she?'

'How could she, indeed!' cried Frances. She thought: It's no good trying to hide it, now.

Lord Broome rubbed his forehead. He looked around the room, as if seeing it for the first time. 'If it's about Richard, I don't think I want to know.'

'You already know. Or at least you have guessed it already.'

He took a gulp of air. She wondered if he were going to faint. There was no colour in his face. He looked worse now than he had looked during the operation. She thought: Let him get used to the idea slowly. She said nothing, nor did she move from the door.

He tried to smile and frown at the same

time. 'You said Richard was ill. That he'd gone to London to get out of Maud's way.'

'It was you who invented that as an excuse for his absence. I would spare you if I could, but it is too late, now. You already know.'

'I know nothing!' he cried out. He was breathing heavily. She thought: I must get help. But she did not move. 'The dogs,' he said. 'No one would have dared to get rid of the dogs unless . . . No, it can't be. Why, he's only a couple of years older than myself. Tell me it is not true, and we will send for the chess set and a newspaper and have a nice quiet morning together.'

'It is true, my lord.'

'Don't call me that. He is not dead. He can't be. Not Richard! Did they get him after all? Was it all for nothing? Why didn't I tell the truth at the inquest!'

CHAPTER SIX

Lord Broome lay as still as if he were already dead. When spoken to, he was deaf; when touched, he did not appear to feel; when food and drink were put to his lips, he refused to partake. He lay on his back with his eyes open, and saw nothing.

Frances was distracted. Theo came and looked grave. He said that his patient had not suffered a stroke, as was Frances' first thought, but that he had simply given up hope. He told Frances that he had seen this sort of thing before and that it was always "worrying". By "worrying", he meant "fatal". Frances understood. Theo suggested that if Frances were unable to rouse Lord Broome, he should be kept warm, given laudanum and left to sleep off the shock.

She watched Theo's face to see if his judgment of his patient's condition were coloured by the feeling he had for his patient's nurse, but all she could read there was concern.

With Theo gone, Frances began to go to pieces. What should she do first? Ought she to leave his lordship, even for an instant, in order to speak to Mrs Broome on her own behalf? Or to Mr Manning on Benson's part? Should she send messages that she wished to speak with them, or write notes? She did not wish to leave Lord Broome, and yet it seemed as if she could do nothing to help him while she was there. She sent for hot bricks and put them in the bed, and wrapped Lord Broome up warmly in her shawl. The agency nurse had been brought back to the sick-room, of course, and punctuated every action with a sniff.

Frances would very much have liked to sit down and weep, but common sense prevented her from doing so. She must act? But in what way?

The nurse tried to get Lord Broome to take a sleeping draught. He refused. Frances tried. Again he refused. And still he stared blankly at the tester above him.

There was a knock on the door. It was Meakins again, all ingratiating smiles and apologies, since she understood that she had inadvertently "let the cat out of the bag", as the saying goes! Frances found it hard to be civil to the woman. Surely Meakins had known? Frances was certain that she had.

The vicar arrived, and said he wished to pray over Lord Broome. Frances explained what had happened. Her weariness and despair were so obvious that the man of God turned from his duty to Lord Broome to comfort Lord Broome's nurse. And Frances was comforted. The time-honoured words rolled round her head and some of them stayed there. She did not oppose the vicar this time when he said he wished to be left alone with the patient.

She was without employment. She walked a few steps down the Gallery and then went back again. In her overwrought state of mind it seemed to her that everything she undertook was fated to end badly. Like Lord Broome, she was a born fighter and her instinct now was to combat her troubles by facing them. But which problem should she tackle first? Should she go first to Mrs Broome or to Mr Manning? Benson might be able to rouse his master, if she could get him released, but that would take time. She ran a few steps towards the gun-room, and then clapped her hands in despair and stopped short. Why had she not thought of it earlier? She ought to have told Theo of the attempt to poison her last night. She ran up to the schoolroom in search of evidence. The fire had not been laid that day, or the bed made, but the tray on which the drink had stood was gone, and so was the half-empty glass from which she had drunk. It was as if she had imagined the whole thing.

She rang the bell. She would start by making enquiries about the drink. No one came. She started to write a note, advising Theo of what had happened. Her hands were so cold . . . she chafed them . . . she would take the paper and ink down to the sick-room where it would be warm, and write her note there. Perhaps she could even enlist the vicar's help.

Half-way down the stairs, she was met by one of the footmen. She was wanted in the gun-room, immediately.

Her mind leaped to the telegram which had come from Bath and she knew, or rather she feared, that this summons related to her past life. Why had she not gone straight to Mrs Broome that morning and confessed all?

Hugo was alone in the gun-room. He was smoking a cigar as usual, and in his hand he held not one, but several telegraph forms. He did not ask her to sit, as he would have done if the interview were to be pleasant.

'A tiresome matter,' said Hugo, looking not at her but at the point of his cigar. 'You are the same Miss Chard who was until recently employed by a Mrs Palfrey of Gloucestershire?' She bowed her head. 'You left your place there without a reference, under suspicious circumstances, and yet you did not see fit to tell my aunt of it?'

'Yes, I acted wrongly. I ought to have spoken of the affair to Mrs Broome, but the subject was still so painful that I shrank from doing so. May I tell you what happened?'

'I have the gist of the affair, I believe. This man—Walter Donne—Mrs Palfrey writes that he has turned out very badly, and has since been cast off by his aunt; that he is reported to be keeping bad company in Town. You still hear from him?'

'No, indeed. I am sorry, for he had many good qualities, and I believed him to be fond of his aunt. No, I have neither seen nor heard anything of him since I left Mrs Palfrey's.'

'But you have his current address?'

'No.'

'I am informed he has taken lodgings in Bayswater.'

'I know nothing of that.'

'I can check with the servants, to see if you have received any letters from him.'

'Do so. You will find nothing.'

'You are almost convincing, Miss Chard.'

'Mr Broome, I am and was innocent of anything but imprudence in allowing Mr Donne to single me out and pay court to me, and even for that I am most heartily sorry.'

He dropped the telegraph forms into the fire. 'I am satisfied. I have not told Mrs Broome about this, and I shall not do so. In view of the services which you are rendering the family, and the heavy responsibility you have undertaken, I think I may safely promise that you have heard the last of this matter. You understand me, I suppose?'

'I am not sure that I do.'

'Come now; you are a clever girl, Miss Chard. I think you understand me very well. Originally the doctors said he wouldn't last the week out. Well, he did and he survived the operation against all odds. But I hear he has now lapsed into a coma. How long do you think he will last?'

'I am not trained to judge. You must ask the doctor. Indeed, I cannot help you.'

'Oh, but I think you must!'

Maud Broome entered the room, without knocking. She looked annoyed to find the despised governess alone with her cousin. She went to Hugo, and linked her arm with his as Frances bobbed a curtsey and left the room.

Spilkins was passing by. 'Where is Mr Manning?' she asked him.

'He's out visiting in the landau with Miss Seld and Mrs Broome. They've gone over to the Armstrongs for a while, but I don't know whether they will be bringing Miss Agnes back with them or not. It depends. Wonderful recoveries Mrs Broome makes when there's a chance of her seeing company.'

'Spilkins, I am in trouble. His lordship is so ill, and the locks on the bedroom doors are faulty. Can you arrange for them to be changed?'

He looked doubtful, but said he would have a message sent down to the smith in the village, who might be able to do something.

Frances sought out Lady Amelia, who was crouched over the fire in the Great Hall, playing patience. Frances felt that she must tell someone—anyone in authority—immediately, everything that she knew and suspected about the goings-on in the sick-room. Also, it was of paramount importance that Benson be rescued from jail. If Mr Manning were not available, then she must try Lady Amelia.

But Lady Amelia was too old and had been too battered by life to be the sort of ally Frances was seeking. She was full of rheumatism and peevish. The wind had moved round so that this chimney smoked, as well. Frances begged the favour of a few minutes' speech. Lady Amelia asked if it couldn't wait till Mrs Broome returned. Frances said no, it couldn't wait, and plunged into her narrative, re-living in her mind every incident as it had occurred. It was some time before she realised that Lady Amelia was regarding her with horrified fascination and disbelief, and then she heard a sarcastic laugh behind her, and her heart sank. Maud and Hugo had come into the hall, and overheard her.

'Really, Miss Chard!' said Maud. 'It is plain that your hours of watching over my cousin have damaged your health.'

'Could any of it be true?' quavered Lady Amelia, but she asked Hugo and not Frances, and Hugo's answer was foreseeable. He gave Frances a look which indicated that he no longer regarded her as a friend, and told her to withdraw to her quarters. She thought: So I am to be dismissed.

She did not attempt to argue, but withdrew. She had tried, and she had failed, and she knew that by the time she reached Mr Manning he would be well primed with the story of her "fantasies". Trust Hugo for that!

She returned to the sick-room, not knowing where else to go. The vicar had gone, but Abel and Polly were sitting, both on the same chair, by the window. Frances asked them to wait outside. She could see at a glance that his lordship had not moved since she left.

When she was alone, she put chairs under the knobs of the doors to ensure privacy. If he was to die, and she to be dismissed, she would at least have one hour with him, quite alone, to remember in the lonely years to come. She climbed on to the bed, and drew him into her arms. He lay limply against her. She put his maimed hand to her lips. Her tears wet his fingers, and tasted salt as she kissed them away. She did not attempt to control them. Had she not cause to cry? When Mrs Broome came back from the Armstrongs, Hugo would see that Frances was dismissed, at once, without a reference. And she would be turned out, and tonight, or perhaps some time late this evening, the "monk" would creep back into the room with a pillow in his hands, and the pillow would be placed over the face of the sleeping man, lying there defenceless, with his batman in jail . . . and there would be an end of Gavin Broome.

And what could she do about it? Discredited, twice dismissed without a reference, she would be laughed to scorn if she attempted to take her story to the police. And even if she were bold enough to do so, by the time she reached Lewes and had told her story there, it would be too late for Gavin Broome. It does not take long to smother a helpless invalid. Five minutes, say. Why, it could be done within half an hour of her leaving the house . . . or even while she was packing her things to go! She clutched him to her, and began to kiss him.

'Wake up! Oh, my darling . . . wake up!'

Did he sigh? Had he moved his head a little, to look at her? His eyes glittered. Had they changed direction? She pushed the hair out

161

of his eyes, and kissed him again, but this time gently. She willed him to awaken. She prayed for him to do so. He sighed. Yes, this time there was no doubt of it. He had lowered his eyelids. He must not slip away from her. She must attract his attention at all costs.

'Benson!' she said, speaking slowly and distinctly. 'He needs your help. He is in jail. I don't know whether they will have put him in irons or not, but at the very least he will be in a cold, damp cell, with a straw pallet to sleep on, which is probably infested. They won't handle him with care, will they? To them, he is a murderer and a thief, scum from nowhere.'

She thought she had his attention. The line between his eyebrows deepened.

'He saved your life,' she said. 'I don't suppose you remember it, but he did. It was the first day I came to see you. He thought you were dead, and he cried. And now they say he tried to kill you, and they've locked him away in jail, and will hang him in due course. Won't you try to help him?'

His lips moved. Had he tried to speak Benson's name? She went on talking, telling him of what Benson had done for him, and of the things he had said to her. Presently he put his good hand over his eyelids and pressed them. He shook his head sharply, as if trying to clear it.

'Nightmares.' His voice was a mere thread. 'So many nightmares. What was real? Richard

. . .' He shook with a nervous chill. She pressed his face to her shoulder and held him, comforting him as she would a child. Presently he was still. He lay back on his pillows, let her wash his face and hands, and took a drink of water.

'Richard,' he said. 'Tell me about him. I didn't dream that, did I? How did they murder him?'

'He wasn't murdered. It was an accident. He took a hedge at the wrong angle, when he was out hunting. I saw the place afterwards. Agnes wanted to see, so we walked up there. He jumped a hedge into Long Acre Field, at a place between two beeches. He came down on a boulder, and it killed him.'

'A boulder in Long Acre Field?' He didn't seem able to absorb the information. 'There are no boulders in Long Acre Field.'

'We saw it. A great big stone, about nine inches across. Not really a boulder, I suppose, but big enough to kill him. It was just a week before he was due to marry Miss Broome. They brought him back, but he didn't recover consciousness. He's buried in the family vault. Listen: about Benson. He was arrested some time yesterday, and is in Lewes jail. They think he attacked and robbed you in the train and stole your money. Someone denounced him in an anonymous letter, and they found some money on him, in a body belt. I seem to remember Benson's saying something about handling money for you, but . . .'

'I remember, now.' His hand trembled as he pressed it to his eyelids again. 'Lewes station. He got me a paper. Yes, of course, he was carrying my money because of the weight, and my being so helpless, one-handed. Twenty-six, maybe twenty-seven sovereigns. I have a memorandum in the breast pocket of the jacket I was wearing, if you can find it. I was in the carriage, waiting for the train to start. They'd said I ought to go to London as soon as I landed to get my arm seen to, but I wanted to get home first. I was uneasy because I hadn't had any letters from home for months, and I . . . a man got into the carriage. No, two men. I didn't look up, but I saw their legs under the newspaper . . . devilish difficult to read *The Times* when you've got one arm in a sling . . . then nothing. Nothing until much later. But I thought that was all a nightmare, born out of fever. Was it real? A big woman, who breathed through her mouth and stank of gin. Pain, in my head and my arm. Being pulled about by that fool Kimpton and another man I didn't recognise. My arm! Then I was so thirsty. I would have sold my soul for a drink of water, but when I got it, it made me vomit. And I was hungry, too. That couldn't have been real, could it? Was I so ill that everything tasted bad?'

'The nurse doctored your food and drink.'

'Why should she do that?'

'I don't know!' wailed Frances. 'Someone wants you dead, but I don't know who it is. I can't believe Lee is responsible for everything, even if he is the "monk".'

His lordship was still trying to remember. 'The nurse . . . something at the back of my mind . . . I can't remember properly, but it must have been real, because you came into it, and you are real. I was asleep, I think. Then I woke up. I couldn't breathe. I straggled. I remember falling and then my arm . . .! Then I heard your voice. I knew it. I don't know how or why, but I recognised it. And everything changed. There was food and drink and the air smelled fresh and I was warm and clean again. Oh, the smell of good soap and fresh sheets and linen. And you. Did you sing to me? It wasn't just a dream, was it? Did you really kiss me? I thought I ought not to ask, in case you had regretted it, since. Only now I don't know what was real and what was not, and I need to know. Did you kiss me?'

'I . . . yes.'

'And just now, too?'

Frances went scarlet. She got off the bed and tidied her hair. 'If I did, it was because you seemed like a child to me.'

'Brazen creature,' said his lordship, with an echo of his old raillery. He settled himself more comfortably on his pillows and looked around him. 'We'll need pen, pink and paper. There won't be any in this room. I'll dictate what I want to say to the police, and sign it, but you'll have to act as witness to my signature.'

'Why? Isn't your word good enough?'

'My handwriting isn't. My signature isn't what it used to be, and I've no signet ring. Richard had one, but I expect it was buried with him.' His right hand clenched, and then relaxed. 'Benson must be cursing me for leaving him in that place. And what about some food? I'm hungry. And the fire has burned low. Where the devil is everyone? And what was that you said about someone other than Lee trying to kill me?'

*   *   *

Although Frances had more than half-expected to be called from the sick-room to receive notice of her dismissal, the rest of the day and that night passed without incident. No member of the family bothered to do more than enquire at the sickroom door how his lordship was doing, and the fiction was preserved that the injured man was sinking fast. This was Lord Broome's doing. He needed time, he said; also he wanted to talk privately to Arling and to his uncle Manning before he was ready to receive his family. All Frances' protests were overruled. As she had guessed, Lord Broome was too set on having his own way to listen to reason.

Theo arrived to see his patient before

Frances had finished telling her tale, and it was he who witnessed Lord Broome's straggling signature and took the statement, with the pocket-book which proved Benson had a right to carry his master's money, away with him. He proposed to leave his practice to take care of itself while he journeyed to Lewes to fetch Benson. It was not thought wise to let this move be widely known in the household, but Lord Broome took Abel and Polly into his confidence and was rewarded by their fervent assurances of support.

Arling was another man Lord Broome took into his confidence. He was with Lord Broome for nearly an hour, and what was said between the two men caused Frances to tremble more than ever for her patient's life. Where would this wickedness end? But she had to confess that she felt happier when Arling sent up a stalwart groom to sit outside the sick-room door; ostensibly he was there so that Frances could send a message to the doctor at any hour of the day and night, but in reality he was acting as a bodyguard. Arling himself took the early night watch, and it was hoped that Benson would be back before midnight.

In the event, neither Theo nor Benson reappeared that night. Lord Broome wondered whether to get out his pistols to put under his pillow, but Arling talked him out of it. Instead, a second burly groom appeared to relieve the man on duty outside the door, and

Frances slept soundly.

It was raining hard when she woke next morning. And still there was no sign of Benson, or of Theo. His lordship staggered to the chair in the window when Frances was in the dressing-room, and laughed in her face when she scolded him. Extra food was smuggled into the sick-room by Polly, and the agency nurse, whom Frances could not trust to hold her tongue about the improvement in his lordship's condition, was told that her services were no longer required. To make sure that she spoke to no one in the household, Arling himself drove her to the station and put her on a train back to Lewes.

An uneasy gaiety ruled the sick-room. His lordship taught Frances the basic moves of chess, and she mended a rent in his dressing-gown. The Court was hushed. Everyone was waiting for something to happen. Agnes was returned by the Armstrongs at tea-time, but her noisy laughter seemed shockingly inapt in the silence that had fallen over the Court. And still it rained, and still there was no sign of Theo or of Benson.

Frances' nerves were getting frayed. Lord Broome demanded a cigar and some wine with his supper. She refused to let him have either, on medical grounds.

'Now let's get this straight,' he said. 'If I want a cigar, or wine, then I shall have it, and you will not treat me as if I were seven

168

years old any longer. Likewise no one—not even you—is to offer to do anything for me, however clumsy I am, unless I actually ask for help. Is that understood?'

Frances nodded.

His lordship relented. 'You would never have made a nurse. You are far too soft-hearted.'

He sent Polly to fetch his uncle, with instructions to speak to Mr Manning when that gentleman was alone and the summons might go unremarked in the household. Polly managed this very well. Frances was sent to walk in the Gallery while Mr Manning was with Lord Broome. She thought she knew why, and the knowledge oppressed her. Was everyone at the Court evil?

Meakins, the ladies' maid, came into the Gallery.

'Have you anything to report, Miss Chard?'

Frances shook her head. She knew what the woman meant. It was plain that she was in Hugo's pay. It was a great comfort to know that no one could get into the sick-room past Arling's man.

Theo and Benson turned up just as she was settling his lordship down for the night. The batman was filthy, and unshaven. He had lost one of his shoes and his clothes were torn.

'Stupid fool to get yourself arrested,' was his master's greeting.

Benson grinned and said he'd be all right

once he'd had a crack at whoever it was that had framed him.

'When you've had a bath, you mean. And eaten, and changed. You may sleep next door when you've made yourself presentable. And I mean sleep, not watch. All that's been taken care of. As for the matter of revenge, you may leave that to me.'

'Pleasure, Major,' said Benson, and went off to horrify the staff in the servants' hall.

*   *   *

Agnes danced into Frances' room next morning while she was dressing. Agnes was anxious to tell her governess everything that she had seen and done while she had been away. She said she had a "big secret" to tell her governess, but before she could do so, Polly knocked on the door to say that Miss Chard was required in the sick-room straight away. Agnes pulled a face, Miss Chard kissed the child, and promised to have a long talk with her later on that day.

Lord Broome was up, shaved, dressed and sitting in the chair by the window with a rug over his knees. He had a pad of paper at his side on which he was painstakingly making notes.

'Frances, we're in trouble. Two policemen have arrived in the village from Lewes, wanting to see me. Whoever it was who wrote that anonymous letter has a lot to answer for. If it hadn't been for that, I might have been able to clear everything up without a scandal. As it is, I shall have to see the police to confirm what I wrote to them and give them as much help as I can about the assault in the train. I wish I could identify the two men positively, but I can't. I know it was Lee and Jervis, but I can't prove it, and I shall have to tell them so.'

'But you can't let them go around making attempts on your life.'

'Believe me, I could have neutralised them without bringing the police into it. At least, I could have done before they murdered Nurse Moon.'

'What was that?'

'Theo identified her body yesterday. That was why he was so long in Lewes. They have a description of the man they think murdered her, and it sounds as if it could be Lee. Theo's been to see me this morning already, to brief me on what's been happening. He's made it clear that I've got to see the police and allow them to issue warrants for the arrest of Lee and Jervis.'

'So why are we in trouble?'

'Because of all the other things that have been going on here, which are family affairs, and have nothing to do with the police. I don't want the police nosing into things which don't concern them, but now that they're here, and unless we're very lucky indeed, the whole sordid story is going to come out. I can't stop them taking Lee and Jervis; on reflection, I suppose I don't really want to. But if I can prevent them taking their investigations any further, I must do so. Now, you will have to see the police. They will want a statement from you about seeing the "monk" in my room. You should stick to the events of that night, and not mention anything else. You understand? Oh, yes, and it will not be necessary to mention that you were in your night-gown at the time. But don't volunteer information about anything else. And now, my dear, before they come, I must speak to my aunt about you.'

She put her hand on his shoulder. 'You will knock yourself up, I know you will. Why not receive your visitors in bed?'

He put his hand over hers and pressed it. 'I've been out of action long enough.'

She withdrew her hand. She thought: It had to come to an end. Once his family come through that door, once they see he is on the road to recovery, once Lee and Jervis have been arrested, my part is done.

Mrs Broome arrived, her shawl trailing on the floor, and her hair untidy. She was astounded to find her nephew so very much alive. She kept repeating that she could not believe it, and yet within a minute she was talking about her own ailments, just as Lord Broome had foretold.

Frances made as if to depart when Mrs

Broome arrived, but his lordship caught her hand.

'Aunt, I really must thank you for making Miss Chard my nurse. She has saved my life several times over. Without her, I would have died, I am sure. I want you to know that I have asked her to be my wife . . .'

Frances interrupted him. 'But I have never said that I would, my lord.'

'Yes. Well.' Mrs Broome appeared uncomfortable in her chair. 'Very understandable, Gavin, although not quite . . . All that glitters is not gold, you know.'

'I agree,' said his lordship. 'But Miss Chard is no imitation. The vicar will probably want to marry us, but I fancy a wedding in the Cathedral, with six bridesmaids. Don't you think Maud and Isabella would enjoy acting as bridesmaids to Frances?'

Frances pulled her hand away and ran out of the room. She had not dreamed he would be so precipitate . . . she had never given him to understand that she would marry him . . . their intimacy had been the result of unnatural circumstances . . . he would soon get over his infatuation . . . he must not ruin himself by allying with a governess, whose past was so . . .

Meakins was waiting for her in the Gallery. Hugo Broome wished to speak to Miss Chard at once, in the Great Hall. She turned to look at the sick-room door. Should she seek sanctuary there? Should she tell his lordship

173

what Hugo intended? No. It was better to end it now, before Lord Broome compromised himself too far. She would accept dismissal without demur.

Hugo was sitting by the fire, smoking, and reading a newspaper.

'You are a very stupid girl,' he said, as soon as she was well within the room. 'You have deliberately thrown your chances away. I was prepared to be your friend and patron, but what do I hear? You have been meddling with affairs that don't concern you. You have dragged the police into what was a purely family matter, and gossiped to the doctor. Did I not warn you?'

Frances said nothing. She felt tired and empty. She knew what was coming and although she dreaded it, she thought it was only right that she should go.

'He is getting better, they tell me,' said Hugo. 'Sitting up, eating properly? Is that true?'

"You must ask the doctor.'

'I am asking the woman I put in charge of the sick-room.'

'Yes, he is better. I think he will recover.'

Hugo threw his cigar into the fireplace. 'I also hear that you have so worked on him that in his weakened state he is prepared to offer you marriage.'

How had he learned these things? By listening at doors? By getting Meakins to listen

174

at doors? By bribing Polly and Abel? No, by bribing one of Arling's men.

'He did ask me to marry him, but I refused. Of course I know that marriage is out of the question.'

'I am glad you realise that, at least. If you did marry him, you would never be received in Society. The story of your involvement with Walter Donne would always go before you. In public, your husband might be acknowledged by his acquaintances, but no one would dare to acknowledge your existence. You could never be presented at Court, and naturally you would not receive any invitations to the houses of families of good reputation. You would cut him off from Society.'

She bowed her head. Would it really have been as bad as that?

He said, 'It would be better if you did not see him again. I am sure you agree.' She shivered, but said nothing. 'Go and pack. Arling will take you to the station. I assume you will return to your aunt's. Your wages will be paid up to date, and your rail ticket bought for you. Please do not attempt to communicate with Miss Agnes or any member of the staff. I have given instructions that the child is to be moved out of the nursery until you have gone, so that she may not be further contaminated by your presence. Nurse will stay with you until it is time for you to leave. That is all.'

She hesitated. 'The police want to see me

before I go.'

Hugo swore. 'Very well. I will try to arrange it that they interview you straight away, so that you may leave this afternoon.'

*　　　*　　　*

There was a tear-stained note in Frances' work-box. "I don't believe it. I'll love you for ever. Agnes." Frances bit her lip. She did not wish Nurse to see her cry. She packed, and sat down in a chair to read. She did not take in the sense of what she saw. Nurse sat at the table, darning; she did not reply when Frances spoke to her. The day wore on. She waited for a summons to see the police, but it did not come. The great house seethed with excitement under and around her; the news was out that Lord Broome had made an astonishing recovery. Frances could hear running footsteps, and the sound of excited laughter. But in the schoolroom all was silent. A footman—not Abel—brought them lunch.

A knock on the door. It was Theo. Nurse hesitated when the doctor signed for her to leave them, but she finally did so. Frances was pleased to see Theo but feared he had come to tell her Lord Broome was worse.

'No,' said Theo. 'He is well enough. But I found him trying to haul himself up the stairs here. He'd been told you were ill, and he wanted to see for himself. I said I'd act as his courier. Oh, yes, and the police want you in ten minutes' time in the gun-room.'

'I'm not sick. I'm leaving this afternoon. Mr Hugo dismissed me. Don't look so upset. It's only right that I should go.' She told him about Mrs Palfrey and Walter and how she could never bear to drag Lord Broome down, when he had already done himself so much damage in the eyes of the world. 'Tell him that I go of my own free will,' she concluded. 'He won't understand at first. Maybe he won't understand for some time. He's inclined to deceive himself into thinking that if he wants something, he's going to get it. He wants me, now; but he'll get over it. He must marry well to retrieve his position in Society.'

'And you?' He took her hand. She did not withdraw it, but shook her head. He sighed. 'Well, you can't leave today, that's for certain. He's commanded us all to appear in the music-room after supper tonight, and that means you, too. He made that very clear. The Armstrongs are invited and the vicar and the family solicitor, and some of the servants. He says he's going to clear up all the irritating little mysteries which have been bedevilling the Court, but we're not to let the police get wind of the meeting. It's to be very private. And so I shall see you again tonight. And, Frances, if you ever change your mind about . . . if you are short of money . . . you know where to find me.'

*   *   *

Polly came up to hook Frances into her black silk evening dress, and drape her black shawl across her shoulders. She had heard that Frances was to leave, and the news had made her unhappy. Frances kissed the little maid before she descended into the Gallery.

Lord Broome was waiting for her, Benson at his side.

Frances' erstwhile patient was resplendent in civilian evening dress. She had cherished the hope that he might appear in uniform because she thought it would have become him, but he had obviously put all military things behind him. His left hand was in a sling. He looked tired and stern.

'Haven't you a dress in any bright colour?' Such was his greeting. 'Turn round.' Frances hid a smile and revolved. 'Well, it will have to do for now. Benson, didn't you get her some more shawls? If she had something in jade green or old gold to wear on that dress, it would look better.'

'No, Major; I haven't had time yet.' Benson grinned at Frances. 'Don't take any notice of him, Miss. He's always fidgety before a battle.'

'I quite understand,' said Frances. 'Some of my children have actually made themselves sick with excitement before a party.'

Lord Broome looked outraged, and then

178

laughed. 'So be it. Frances, give me your arm. I don't want to make my entrance into the music-room by falling down the stairs.' As they walked slowly to the end of the Gallery, he lowered his voice. 'You don't really mean to leave me, do you? You don't have to take any notice of what Hugo says; his reign is over. But you knew that. You are not such a weakling that you had to take his orders quietly.'

'I am not going to marry you, to drag you down. Nor will I take advantage of the infatuation of a man who has been dangerously ill.'

'Do I detect the fine Italianate hand of my cousin Hugo at work? Wherever he goes, he causes trouble. Do you know, the first time he came to stay, he broke a window and blamed it on a gardener's boy. The boy was dismissed and Hugo commended for having discovered the culprit. Richard gave Hugo a black eye, and I got father to reinstate the gardener's boy. Do you know who that boy grew up to be? It's Abel. It was he who brought me the news of your "illness". Promise me something; promise you'll not go until we've had time to talk this over. What good would it do if you did run away, anyway? I'd only come after you. Do you really think a man of thirty-four doesn't know what he's doing when he proposes marriage?'

Another minute and she might have promised, and avoided much misery for both of them. But they were in the anteroom, and Spilkins was throwing open the double doors at the head of the steps down into the music-room.

The room seemed crowded. Theo appeared at Lord Broome's elbow, to help him down the steps. 'They're all here,' said Theo, sotto voce. 'And I hope to God you're not going to fag yourself out, old man, for they'll be a tough lot to convince. A grimmer set of faces you never did see.'

'The police?' said Lord Broome, also under his breath. 'They won't interfere?'

'They're at the Furze Arms for the night. I've got a man watching them. If they leave, we'll be informed. They got Jervis all right, but I'm afraid Lee slipped through their fingers.'

Then they were nearing the fireplace, and the ranks of the family were solid before them. Hugo, standing beside Mrs Broome and Lady Amelia; Mrs Armstrong, that arbiter of society; the vicar was standing with the General; Mr John Manning was leading Isabella to a seat, while Maud stood beside a strange man in the oriel window.

A large high-backed chair had been placed to one side of the fireplace, and Lord Broome sank into this. Theo smilingly indicated that Frances take a chair near Lord Broome, and took one at her side. Benson had withdrawn to stand guard on the door which led up to the ante-room, because Spilkins had gone to stand with the other servants by the door which led to the dining-room. Frances saw that Arling, Polly and Abel were among those present, and then Lord Broome cleared his throat.

'Mrs Armstrong, General; I am delighted you were able to come at such short notice. Mr Cotton—may I introduce you to Miss Chard? Frances, Mr Cotton is our family solicitor and very welcome on such an occasion. Do take a chair, everybody. Aunt, godmother, cousins all, please find seats. Forgive me if I get down to business straight away. I have much to say and little strength to do so.'

'If you are sure you want to go through this, Gavin,' said Mr Manning. He looked worried. 'The police . . .'

'Have got Jervis, but not Lee. They will no doubt continue in the neighbourhood until they do apprehend Lee. I want to clear up all the other mysterious things that have been happening here before they start to get curious. I do not mean to obstruct justice. There are more than enough of you here to constitute a jury . . .'

'Not so,' interjected the General. 'Women. Not competent, you know.'

'In this case, I think they are,' said Lord Broome. 'Bear with me, please. I am going to put my case, and then I will leave it to you to decide what action ought to be taken. If you decide to turn the matter over to the police, I

181

will offer them my full cooperation.'

'Highly irregular,' said Mr Cotton, speaking for the first time. He was a sandy-haired man with precise features. 'However, I gather that your idea is to avoid airing certain—ah—unpleasant features of the case in public. Naturally, I would be in agreement with such a course.'

'It does seem odd,' quavered Mrs Broome. 'You mean that you want us to be both judge and jury in your own case?'

'Dear aunt,' smiled Lord Broome. 'How acute you can be on occasion, especially where your own interests are involved.'

No one else had anything to say, though one or two people looked as if they would have liked to object, if they could have found the right words in which to do so.

'Then I will begin,' said Lord Broome, 'with my brother Richard. He was in many ways a lovable man, but he was flawed. He was brought up in the belief that he deserved the best of everything, and that if that cost money, then money would somehow be forthcoming to gratify his whim. I was partly to blame in fostering this delusion. Like him, I thought it not entirely fair that I had inherited the whole of my great-uncle's fortune, and I was only too happy to help Richard out when he got into financial difficulties. Richard was also flawed in another way. You will forgive me, ladies, if I refer to a matter not usually mentioned in

182

mixed company, but it was an open secret that Richard was not as perfectly made as a man might be. If he had only had the courage to go to a doctor who specialised in such cases, if Dr Kimpton had not been so sure that Richard was impotent, none of this would have happened. Or perhaps it would. There were other people involved . . .

'Richard came to manhood believing himself set apart from mankind. He avoided the company of women, and urged me to marry to carry on the line. Maybe I would have done so, if I had met the right woman, but it did not seem urgent, and so time passed until I came home last summer on leave. Richard was no penman, and I had had maybe two letters from him in the previous two years, both of which contained requests for money. That does not mean that he had lost his affection for me. He was delighted to see me, and within twenty-four hours of my return he had told me his great secret—he had found a woman who loved him, and who was pregnant by him. The flaw which had kept him a monk for so many years proved to be utterly unimportant, and he felt a new man. I believe I congratulated him,' said his lordship with a thin smile. 'I certainly did not reprove him, or enquire the details of his liaison. He had not mentioned marriage. I assumed, rightly as it happened, that the woman was already married. The affair certainly seemed to have done him a lot of good. For the first time he was able to speak to women without blushing. Oh, he was still shy in their presence, but he had ceased to avoid their company. I was very struck by the way his eyes followed Maud when she came into a room, and equally struck by the way her eyes sought his. My aunt had long wished Maud to marry one of us, and it was only natural that Maud should take advantage of Richard's changed outlook on women. Before I could counsel caution, Richard asked me to congratulate him on his forthcoming marriage. Naturally, I did so. Richard was so happy that I could not bear to ask him whether he was sure Maud returned his regard in equal degree.'

Maud turned in her chair to look at Hugo. He, however, sat with his eyes on Lord Broome, and did not appear to have noticed her movement.

'When the engagement was announced, Lilien Jervis came up to the Court with the idea of making things unpleasant for my brother. Richard was out, so she asked to see me instead. I agreed, without realising that it was she with whom Richard had been having an affair.

'As soon as she walked into the room, I guessed what had been going on. I had not seen her before. I had been away for a couple of years, if you remember, and she was not a local girl. Her mother kept a small shop in a village some five miles away. Lilien's father was half a gypsy and used to go off on his own for months at a time, tramping the countryside, plying his tinker's trade, but the girl had been brought up strictly by her mother. In many ways, Lilien was right to have ambitions above her station. She had a smattering of education, her manners were good, and she was, of course, magnificent to look at. She had met Jervis at a fair, had been intrigued by the thought of the contact with "the gentry" which Jervis could offer her. She was troublesome at home, so her mother was only too glad to marry the girl off. She was only sixteen, poor child, and she thought Jervis was offering her the keys to the Gates of Heaven. Marriage to him did not bring content. He failed to get her pregnant, and after a while she grew to despise him and look for satisfaction elsewhere. Her eye had fallen on my brother, and she had seduced him with results which had seemed at first to be satisfactory all round. He could not visit her at the lodge, so he gave her two keys; one to the postern door which lets you into the courtyard from the park, and one to the door of his dressing-room. He always locked his bedroom door at night. Lilien would creep up through the shrubbery, circle the outbuildings until she came to the postern, and go through that into the cloisters. The only time she was in danger of being seen was in the cloisters, on the stairs, or in the Gallery. Richard obtained a white monk's robe for her to wear, which she used to keep hidden behind some logs in one of the store-rooms below. Thus it was that the legend of our family ghost was reborn, and the cloisters and Gallery became a place to be avoided after dark.

'I think she loved him; certainly she ran great risks for him. Jervis did not take lightly to being cuckolded, but he put up with it until she told him that she was bearing Richard's child. It was early days with her. She could have concealed her pregnancy for some time, but Richard had just announced his engagement to Maud, and she thought the time had come to put her cards on the table. She did not want to be stuck in the village for the rest of her life. She wanted something better for herself and her child. Richard could not marry her, but he could set her up "as a lady" in Lewes, with a maid to wait on her and plenty of money to buy clothes with. That was why she came up to the Court. There was anger and jealousy as well, but basically she wanted what she called "her rights".

'As I said before, Richard was out that day. I suggested to Lilien that she return to her mother's, and that I would get Richard to contact her there. She said she dared not. Gypsies have a rigid code of honour where their women are concerned and punish their adulterers severely. She feared what her father might do to her, if she went back home. She could not, of course, go back to Jervis. That was out of the question. So I sent her with a note to my mother's old maid who lives a couple of miles off in the opposite direction to Lilien's birthplace, asking her to take the girl in for the time being. Then I consulted Richard as to what was to be done. He had no ideas on the subject. I suggested that the matter be placed in the hands of Mr Cotton, and that he should arrange things . . .'

'This is all very well,' said Hugo. 'But it's easy to place the blame on Richard, now that he's dead and can't contradict you . . .'

'If you please!' said Mr Cotton. He looked annoyed. 'I can bear out everything that this witness—I mean Lord Broome—says. The two brothers came to see me at my office about the affair. The late Lord Broome was concerned that no word of the matter should reach his fiancée, but he very properly wanted to do what was right for Mrs Jervis and her child. I suggested that money be found to send Mrs Jervis to another part of the country, or even abroad. This was agreed to. The present Lord Broome offered to put up the money since his brother was always short of funds. When Mrs Jervis moved to Lewes, I visited her on several occasions to discuss the matter of the child's upbringing, which . . .'

'Softly,' said Lord Broome. 'You are going too fast. Before Mr Cotton could finalise arrangements, Richard received a verbal message that Lilien wished to speak with him.

Her father and husband had found out where she was, had dragged her from the cottage and beaten her. They wanted her to tell them who was responsible for her plight. She would not tell. They had guessed that it was one of us, because we had sheltered her, but they did not know which. Richard's reputation was against his being responsible, and I had not been home long enough. So they beat her. They were interrupted, and fled. Richard got the girl cleaned up and sent her to Lewes, where Mr Cotton visited her, as he says.'

'That is so,' said Mr Cotton. 'And I cannot express my disapproval of your subsequent conduct strongly enough, my lord. If you had only called me as a witness at the inquest . . .'

'Again, you are jumping the gun,' said Lord Broome. 'The girl was settled in Lewes, Richard was happily showering Maud with gifts, and I was pursuing matrimony on my own account. Then Richard received a letter from Lilien. Her father and husband had once more discovered where she was living. They had not yet approached her, but were having her watched. She had not seen Richard for some time. She was lonely and in great distress, and she wanted to be reassured that nothing was going to happen to her or her baby. She reminded Richard that she still had his keys, and she asked him to meet her at dusk the following evening in the park by the footbridge. She said that Mr Cotton had

188

promised to hand over her passage money to America the following day, and that she would never trouble Richard again, if only she could see him just once before she left. Richard asked me to accompany him to the rendezvous, partly as a chaperone in case Maud should see him meeting another girl, and partly as a bodyguard in case Jervis or Lee should turn up.

'I agreed, the more fool I. We were a little late. We could see her running towards the footbridge, on the other side of the river, as we rode up. She had a red shawl around her, and her hair had come loose under her bonnet. Ordinarily she was fleet of foot, but she was pregnant and the men—Jervis and Lee—were both fit. They were gaining on her. We could not take the horses across the bridge; it was not safe. We dismounted, and I tethered the horses while Richard ran towards the bridge. I thought the men would stop chasing her when they saw us, but they didn't. There was a mist coming up, and no one else in sight. Lee caught up with his daughter and started to drag her back the way she had come. She freed herself after a sharp struggle, and left him on the ground while she ran on. She left her shawl behind her. We could see she was holding a knife, and that the blade was dark. Lee was nursing one shoulder, and his coat sleeve was dark, too. She reached the far end of the bridge just as Richard stepped on to his

189

end. She was panting. She held the knife to her breast. Richard cried out, to warn her that Jervis was close behind her. She turned and caught her foot, and before Jervis could reach her, or Richard . . . she fell against the handrail and it snapped . . . and she went down into the water.'

CHAPTER SEVEN

Someone sighed. A ripple of movement went through the company. Lord Broome leant back in his chair and momentarily closed his eyes. Theo leant forward and set a glass of cordial at his patient's right hand. Lord Broome sipped it, and set it down again.

'She didn't have a chance. The water was high and running smoothly. She was wearing a dark dress. We looked for her, but didn't see her. Jervis and I both dived in to look for her. We failed. Richard was dazed. He kept saying that he'd told them to mend the bridge months ago. After a while Lee struggled up, his coat sodden with blood. He said we were looking in the wrong place for her, and that she'd come up in the lower pool. I don't know how he knew. Probably he'd been poaching there. There she was, all right, floating face down. We got her out, but she was dead. There was a bruise on her forehead which hadn't been there when she fell, and we thought she must have hit her head on one of the struts when she passed under the bridge, been knocked out, and drowned. She looked peaceful enough, poor girl.'

He looked around at the company. 'Well, what would you have done, in my place? Richard begged me to cover for him; he was afraid that Maud would break off their engagement if the truth were to come out. Jervis sat there, weeping, because the woman he'd loved and married was dead. Lee was drained of blood, hardly able to stand, mourning his only child. Perhaps I ought to have allowed the whole thing to come out, to let everyone take their share of the blame, but it seemed unnecessary. I told Jervis to take Lee back with him, to be nursed back to health. I sent Richard back to the Court, waited half an hour, and then raised the alarm. At the inquest I told the truth, but not the whole truth. If I had called Mr Cotton to give evidence, if anyone had thought to ask Dr Kimpton how many months the girl had been pregnant, the coroner might have felt impelled to urge that further enquiries should be made as to how the girl died. My object was to get the matter over and done with. Now I ask you, ladies and gentlemen of the jury, was the coroner's verdict correct?'

'Misadventure,' said Mr Cotton, 'was the correct verdict, technically.'

191

'Dammit,' said the General, 'I'd have done the same myself, in your place. If only we'd known!'

There was a chorus of agreement.

'That was the object of the exercise,' said Lord Broome, 'That no one should know. Unfortunately, people put the wrong construction on what they heard, and came to the conclusion that I was responsible not only for the girl's pregnancy, but also for her death. Mrs Armstrong cut me, and the girl I had thought to marry intimated that she no longer thought me "reliable". I was given the cold shoulder in public, and in private I was told that the sooner I rejoined my regiment, the better.

'To do him justice, Richard was very upset about this, but I persuaded him not to speak out. I thought the affair would soon be forgotten, once I had gone and Richard was married to Maud. And there I might have been right, if Lee and Jervis had let well alone. I had warned Richard to get rid of them. I had left him enough money to set Jervis up as a tenant farmer in another part of the country, and told him to get Mr Cotton to warn Lee off. I don't know what Richard used the money for, but . . .' He shrugged. 'He allowed things to carry on as they were, and so he died, too.'

'Now, come!' said Hugo. 'Your illness has turned your brain.'

Lord Broome lifted his hand. 'We have

witnesses here who are competent to judge the cause of my brother's death. General, you were out with the hunt that day, and I am told that you were the first to reach my brother after he took his toss. What did you see?'

'A poacher feller sneaking away under the hedge. Didn't recognise him, but then—wouldn't. Got his back to me. Big fellow, moleskin trousers. Thought he'd startled Richard's horse as he jumped the hedge. Horse threw Richard, and broke its own legs. Damn shame. But accident. Nothing to be gained by talking about it. If I'd been quick enough to catch that feller, he'd have heard something from me about it, I can tell you.'

'How long was it before you reached Richard, after you saw him jump the hedge?'

'Coupla minutes. Musta been. I went round by the gate. Couldn't see Richard ahead of me. Looked round. There he was, down. Nothing to be done.'

'You have seen many men die in your time. In some ways you are as great an expert on wounds and dead men as the doctor here. In your opinion, what caused my brother's death?'

'Why, the fall . . . oh, I see what you mean. Falling like that, you usually break your neck, or if the horse rolls on you there's internal injuries. No, nothing like that. The horse was some distance off; couldn't move, you know. Richard had fallen head first on to a stone, struggled up, and then gone down again. Knew that by the way the blood was flowing down over his face . . . pardon, ladies . . . gruesome sight. Best not mentioned. He wasn't dead, but next thing to it.'

'Doctor, your verdict?'

'I saw what the General saw—not the poacher, of course—and deduced the same things. There was blood and hairs on the stone. The stone had come into contact with his head, and it was this injury which caused his death. It was tough luck that such a big stone—almost a boulder—was lying there, just where he fell. If it hadn't been for that, I doubt if there would have been much damage done.'

'Quite,' said his lordship. 'That stone ought not to have been there. That field had just been ploughed. It's good earth there, and not at all stony. As soon as I heard about the stone, I began to wonder about my brother's death. I set myself to work out how I, if I had had any reason to wish to kill my brother, might have managed it. Arling!'

The head groom came out of the knot of servants to stand before him.

'Yes, my lord. Following your instructions, I went up to the field this morning with two witnesses and inspected the trunk of both beech trees. Both showed signs of having been ringed, probably with wire, at about knee height. Later, I took one of the policemen up there and showed him what I'd seen. I also showed him the stone, which had been tossed in the hedge. He agreed with me that there was no other stone anywhere near, anything like it. We then went on up to the top pastures and looked at the stones there. To the best of our judgment, the stone which killed Lord Richard came from the top pastures.'

'And what about my brother's horse?'

'Taking a tumble over a hedge will sometimes break a horse's legs, but these were slashed across and broken, which was strange. I believe that a length of wire was tied to one of the trees, and belayed round the other; that the man standing behind one of the trees jerked the wire up to knee height as Lord Richard jumped the hedge, thus catching the horse's legs and bringing horse and rider to the ground.'

'And then,' said Lord Broome, 'while Richard was struggling to his feet, he was attacked, and hit on the head from above with a large stone which had been brought to that place for that very purpose. There wasn't much time. The General was approaching. But one or two blows would have sufficed. Then the man gathered up his wire and slunk away under the hedge, leaving Richard to die.'

There was a long silence, broken at length by Maud. She was very pale, and her hands trembled as they strayed over the velvet arm of her chair.

'Do you mean Richard was murdered

by Lee or Jervis? Because he bedded that common slut?' She clutched at her throat, and retched, turning her head away from the company.

'The poor thing,' cried Isabella, running to Maud. 'You shouldn't have broken it to her like that.'

'Oh, I don't think Maud is upset because she loved Richard,' said his lordship, his voice as hard as ever.

'Leave me alone! I'll be all right!' Maud beat her cousin's hand away. Her skin was greenish-white, but she was under control.

'What a devilish thing!' said the General, pulling at his moustache. 'And the police know about it? I wonder if I'd recognise the chap again.'

'I daresay the police will give you an opportunity tomorrow,' said Lord Broome. 'They've already arrested Jervis, and are looking out for Lee. I think they'll talk. The problem is, how much will they say? We know they vowed vengeance on the House of Broome. I believe they murdered my brother. I believe that they were also responsible for the four attempts on my life . . .'

'Four attempts?' gasped Mrs Armstrong.

'Proof!' demanded Hugo.

Mr Cotton interrupted. 'May I ask a question? I assume that you would call the attack on the train the first attempt. Neither you nor Benson are able positively to identify your assailants. Circumstantial evidence may point to Jervis and Lee, but did they in fact have an opportunity to carry out the crime? How did they know you were to be on that train?'

'That's easy. I announced my return by telegram, giving the time of the train on which I expected to arrive. Of course Jervis would hear of it. You would have expected him to be at his post on the morning his new master was expected back home, wouldn't you? And yet police enquiries have shown that Jervis asked a cousin of his, one of the gamekeepers, to substitute for him that morning, complaining of toothache. He said he would have to go into Lewes that day to get his molar attended to, and he returned to his post only after I had been carried unconscious past the lodge up to the Court. Someone will have seen him or maybe both Jervis and Lee, either going to Lewes first thing on the morning of my return, or waiting about on Lewes station for me to arrive, or returning to Furze Halt later that day. Does anyone dispute the conclusion I have drawn from these facts?'

No one did.

'Now let us consider the second attempt on my life—by poison. A very different affair, this, or so it seems at first sight. I was not properly conscious for some time after my return. I rejected the food and drink which was given me because they made me sick. I was nursed by strangers, and one of them was responsible for adulterating everything I had to eat and drink with a noxious yellow substance. For the presence of this substance I can bring many witnesses, including Spilkins, Miss Chard, Benson and Abel. But for a change in the manning of the sick-room I would have died of starvation, and no one would have thought anything of it.'

'I don't understand,' said Hugo. 'The doctors got the nurses from an agency in Lewes. It is true that one of the nurses proved incompetent—drunk on duty—and was discharged. There was some talk of her trying to smother you, but that was merely a figment of your servant's imagination. Benson was overtired.'

'Don't forget that Miss Chard also saw that incident. But for her, I would have died either of starvation or of suffocation. Like the doctor and the General, she saw that something was not quite right, but lacking background information, failed to draw the right conclusions—at least for some time.'

'I am sure we all owe much to Miss Chard,' said Mrs Broome insincerely, 'But, Gavin dear, aren't you letting your own imagination run away with you? It was proved that the woman drank, but why should she put something horrid in your food?'

'She was bribed to do so, I suppose. Later still, this same yellow substance made the other agency nurse too ill to assist in an important operation on my arm, and still later it was given to Miss Chard in an effort to keep her out of the way while yet another attempt was made on my life. Which means that the yellow substance passed from the hands of the discredited and dismissed Nurse Moon into the hands of someone who remained here, at the Court.'

'Do you mean,' said Hugo, who seemed short of breath, 'To accuse me of trying to poison you? I assure you that I . . .'

'No, that is not your style. It was very much in your interest that I should not survive, but you are too careful a man to commit a murder, or to bribe others to murder on your behalf, especially by means that can be traced, like the yellow powder. I did toy with the idea of your having bribed the nurse to suffocate me, but on the whole I don't think you were responsible for that. It would be too much to believe that she had been bribed by two people in this house, at one and the same time. No, I think you did little beyond hint this and that to Miss Chard, and to send the telegram to the wrong man when a surgeon was needed. I don't think you actively participated in any of the attempts to murder me, nor do I think you were responsible for forging the Will leaving everything to Maud.'

'Forging?'

'What was that?' Everyone was talking

199

at once, except for Maud and Mrs Broome. Maud's eyes were dilated, and both her hands were pressed to her bosom. Mrs Broome cried out and then stuffed her handkerchief into her mouth. She looked terrified.

'Well, Uncle?' said Lord Broome. 'I believe you suspected what was going on even before I heard about the second Will that I was supposed to have made. Would you like to give us your opinion on the matter?'

Mr Manning stood up, and went to stand with his back to the fire.

'I first began to suspect that the second Will was a forgery when I had time to consider how unlike Gavin it was to forget to leave his brother anything. Gavin had no idea that Richard had been killed when he made this second Will, so why had he not left him any money? That he should have cut Isabella out of his Will was understandable, and it was even understandable that he should have wished to remember his penniless cousins Maud and Agnes in his Will, even though he had not done so before. But to leave everything to Maud, without mentioning Agnes, or Richard, or his faithful servant Benson seemed incredible. Yet the Will undeniably fulfilled all legal criteria; the signatures of the witnesses were apparently those of some of Gavin's brother officers, as they would be if the Will had been made when he was out at the Cape.

'My attention became focused on the date

of the Will. Gavin was wounded at Majuba on January 29th, and has been unable to write with his left hand ever since. His present signature, written with his right hand, is not much like his previous efforts. So how did it come that this second Will was dated in February of this year, and bore Gavin's usual signature?'

'I feel ill!' moaned Mrs Broome.

'The Will dropped out of the Bible which was on a table at the side of Gavin's sick-bed. Later on I made an opportunity of inspecting the books which Gavin keeps at his bedside more closely. In each of these Gavin has inscribed his signature—his old signature—and in two of these books I found notes from brother officers . . . a scrawled invitation to dine, and a note confirming an appointment. One of Gavin's old signatures, and both the signatures from fellow officers seemed to me to be indented on the page. I inspected these signatures under a magnifying glass, and found that they had been gone over with a pointed instrument, but there was no corresponding indentation on the pages underneath. I concluded that someone had traced Gavin's signature on to another piece of paper, and that this was probably how the second Will had come to bear the appropriate signatures. As soon as Gavin was well enough to see me, I brought up the subject of his second Will, and he categorically denied ever having made it.'

Mrs Broome rose from her seat and looked around her as if wondering whether she could leave the room without being prevented from doing so.

'Sit down, Aunt,' said his lordship. 'Little did you know it at the time, but by taking the desk set from this room into the State Bedroom—you had remembered that Richard had neither pen nor paper in his room, hadn't you?—you did me a very good turn. You saved my life, in fact. You dropped a stopper from an inkwell, it rolled half under my bed, and Agnes found it—which brought Miss Chard to my room. I dread to think what might have happened to me if Miss Chard had not entered my room that day.'

'No . . . proof,' panted Mrs Broome. 'The Will . . . destroyed!'

'I'm sure it is. I feel for you, Aunt. You went to all that trouble to ensure your daughter's future and then Miss Chard nursed me so well that I didn't die, after all. You knew that the moment I heard about the Will, I would denounce it, so you took the easy way out. Before the Will could be disputed, you removed it from the bureau in which Hugo had improvidently placed it, and destroyed it.'

Mrs Broome's face crumpled. 'Oh dear, oh dear! What will become of me?'

'Nothing very bad, Aunt. If nobody here has any objection, I propose to allow the matter of the forged Will to rest. There is no proof now that the Will ever existed, and, as Mr Cotton knows, I propose to sign an entirely different Will tomorrow morning. When the Court has a new mistress, I believe my aunt will wish to retire to the Dower House. She is already in receipt of a small pension from the estate, and I will see that it is maintained for life. For her sake—for everyone's sake—I propose that no word of this goes beyond these four walls. Do you all agree?'

Everyone present agreed, but none of them looked at Mrs Broome as she wept in her chair. 'I didn't mean to harm anyone,' she said. 'I wouldn't have done anything actually to harm you, Gavin; believe me.'

'Oh, I believe you,' he said.

'Then, if it wasn't Hugo, and it wasn't Louisa,' said Mrs Armstrong, 'Who was it who was trying to kill you? Inside the house, I mean. There were the two men outside—Jervis and Lee—but who was it inside?'

'Shall we put it another way?' said his lordship. 'Who had access to Dr Kimpton's bag? Theo, will you explain.'

'A powerful emetic, yellow in colour, is missing from my uncle's bag. It is a preparation of ipecacuanha, chamomile and mustard. My uncle has a set of bottles in his bag of different sizes, and this one is missing. He is not well enough to be with us tonight, but when I asked him about the bottle, he said he believed he missed it after one of his visits to Mrs Broome in her apartments.'

'Are you accusing me?' said Isabella, reddening. 'It is true that I looked in Dr Kimpton's bag one day. He'd left it open on the table in Aunt's sitting-room, and I wondered if he had anything for a wart on my little finger.'

'Do you have a guilty conscience, too, Isabella?' said his lordship. 'You stood to gain by my death, but I don't think it was you who masterminded the attacks on my life. You don't possess the strength to bend men like Jervis and Lee to your will.'

'He means me,' said Maud. She was smiling, but still pale. 'He thinks I was poisoning him for the sake of the money I was going to get under his Will. Of course, he is wrong. The new Will did not turn up until long after his return, and some considerable time after he had started to reject food. I defy him to produce a motive.'

'That is easy. You never cared for Richard, and if you grieved at his death it was because you had lost your chance of becoming Lady Broome. My return affected you little one way or the other, but once Hugo had entered the picture you had a very good motive for getting rid of me. Perhaps for the first time in your life you found you could love a man; as a bonus you learned you were to be my heir. You wanted me dead so that Hugo could succeed and marry you. It was you who stole

Dr Kimpton's emetic, first to use on me, then on the agency nurse and lastly on Miss Chard. It was you who stole the money Richard had left in the bureau in the gun-room; you needed money to pay your accomplices. It was you who bribed the nurse and, although it was not you who killed her, it was you who directed that she should be silenced. A drunken woman could not be relied upon to hold her tongue for ever, could she? It was you who stole the housekeeper's and Richard's keys to ensure that you could obtain access to my rooms or to the bureau at any time. It was you who wrote the letter denouncing Benson, so as to get him out of the way while the fourth and last attempt was made on my life.'

'Are you trying to say that I went around the house in a monk's gown, frightening the life out of the servants? What nonsense!'

'No, that was Lee. You remember the keys which Lilien was going to hand back to Richard on the day she was drowned? They were not found on her body, and we assumed they were lost in the river. I think now that Lee snatched them from Lilien when he grappled with her on the river bank. Or maybe she dropped them in the scuffle, and he picked them up later. Lee—or possibly one of his contacts within the Court—found the robe, and saw how useful it could be. He had keys, he had the robe, and he had accomplices within the Court, so he entered my rooms as and when he wished. It was only through the vigilance of Benson and Miss Chard that I was saved from death at his hands.'

'You think . . . you really think that I would consort with a man who had killed my fiancé?'

'I don't think you knew that he had. I think that it was the realisation that you had allied yourself with Richard's murderer which caused you to change colour just now, and to feel faint. How Lee must have laughed when you went to him with suggestions as to how he might carry his vendetta against the House of Broome to its conclusion! You played into his hands, didn't you?'

'What nonsense! I defy you to prove a single word of what you have said.'

'I don't have to. The police will do it for me. They are returning tomorrow to search the Court, and they will bring enough men with them this time to do the job properly. They will take samples of your handwriting . . .' Maud started. '. . . to compare with the note which denounced Benson. I believe that if a search were to be made of your room at the moment, the police would find two bunches of keys, a bottle of emetic, some of the money stolen from the bureau, and perhaps also my aunt's bracelet.'

Mr Manning frowned. 'Gavin, I do not wish to teach you your business, but if what you say is true—and unpalatable though it is, I do not deny that your theory seems to

206

explain everything—then surely you are giving Maud an opportunity to get rid of everything which might incriminate her, before the police arrive?'

Maud threw back her head and laughed.

'Very true, Uncle,' said Lord Broome. 'That is precisely what I am doing. If Maud will admit that the game is up, if she will agree to sign a statement admitting her guilt and give it to Mr Cotton, then I in turn will make her a modest allowance provided that she leaves the Court tomorrow morning and never returns or attempts to communicate with us again. If she will do this, the matter need never be made public. Lee and Jervis will stand trial for their attempts on my life, and the matter of the emetic and of the letter denouncing Benson will remain as unsolved mysteries on the police file. Maud's intentions were murderous, but she has not in fact succeeded in anything she attempted to do, and it will be punishment enough for her to lose not only Hugo, but her chance of becoming Lady Broome. I have never cared for her, but I have some affection for my aunt, and even more for Agnes. I would not wish either of them to undergo the humiliation of seeing Maud stand trial.'

Maud sprang to her feet, her hands clenched. She smiled and smiled, and, cat-like, controlled her movements to lean against the mantelpiece. Her uncle moved away from her, as if unable to bear her proximity. Her smile widened. Incredibly, she yawned.

'My dear Gavin, it is plain that your powers of reasoning have been affected by your illness. I agree that I wished you dead, but then so did most of us, if the truth were only told. I agree that I wrote that note denouncing Benson; the man was obviously guilty, to my mind. If I was mistaken, then I apologise. As for what you call my "alliance" with men such as Jervis and Lee—that is all in your sick mind. You are a very sick man, cousin, are you not? If a drunken woman stole Dr Kimpton's emetic and dosed your food with it, what is that to me? And if someone killed her afterwards, I daresay they had a good reason for doing so—she must have been easy prey for a casual thief. No, your mind has become so clouded by illness that you have entirely overlooked the one real criminal in our midst. Did she not come here with false references? Did she not have a motive to cause confusion in the house? Did she not procure the dismissal of one—if not both—of the agency nurses provided by the doctors? And insinuate herself into the sick-room? Has she not so worked on you that you are prepared to throw yourself and your money at her feet? Who stands to gain from this but Miss Chard?'

'You lie!' cried Frances, rising to her feet. 'My lord—you know my mind in this matter. I have not given you any cause to think that I would marry you. I am leaving as soon as I am permitted to do so. I would have left today but that the police—and then you—required my presence . . .'

'You would have left today. Yes. To go to your lover! Oh, didn't you know, Gavin? I see you turn pale at the very thought that she might have a secret lover.' She looked at the clock on the mantel. It was a few minutes past the hour of nine. 'Spilkins! I believe you will find that a gentleman has just arrived from the station. You may ask him to join us, if you will.'

'What gentleman?' asked the General.

'You have talked a great deal about proof,' said Maud to his lordship. 'I will give you all the proof you need.'

The double doors leading to the dining-room opened, and a man in evening dress sauntered through.

'Walter!' gasped Frances. 'What on earth are you doing here?'

Frances' one-time suitor bowed. He was a well set-up young man of the same physical type as Lord Broome, but younger. Frances shuddered. Once she had considered Walter handsome, but now she read viciousness in his features. The months since she had last seen him were marked on his face in dark shadows round his eyes, a nervous twitch of a muscle in his cheek, and extra weight.

'Good evening, all,' said Mr Walter Donne, fingering his moustache. 'No need to keep up

209

the play-acting, Frances, my dear. We've been rumbled. Miss Broome here knows what we've been up to. The game is up. U for useless, and P for played out. So get your hat and coat on, and we'll be making tracks for the great Metropolis, as planned.'

'I don't understand,' said Frances. 'What game? What plan? I swear to you,' and she knelt at Lord Broome's side and clung to his hand, 'that I have not seen this man, or corresponded with him, since he betrayed me. It is true that I am leaving, but that is for your sake, not mine. I could not bear it if you were hurt through me.'

'I believe you.' Lord Broome was calm, but his voice was a whisper. His skin looked waxen. She pressed her cheek to his maimed hand and then stood, her body shielding him from the rest of the company. 'Can you not see what you are doing to him? He is tired. After what he has been through this evening, to attack him through me is cruel. Can you not leave him alone?'

'It is you who are harming him, not us,' said Maud. 'You have said so yourself. You have admitted that you planned to leave. What you didn't say was that you didn't plan to go alone—or without something to recompense you for all your trouble.'

'My wages,' said Frances. 'That is all. Mr Hugo promised me some money once, but that was only if I should agree to kill Lord Broome, and I did not agree. There is nothing you can hold against me.'

Walter moved forward and tried to take Frances' hand. She struck it away, but he did not falter. 'Come, my dear—what's the use? I've already admitted to Miss Broome that I got the fifteen guineas you sent me a week ago, and very useful it was; although, of course, nothing like the sum we expected to get for the bracelet.'

'The bracelet?' Mrs Broome struggled up from her chair. 'Do you mean that it was you who stole my bracelet, you wicked girl?'

'I have not set eyes on your bracelet from the moment you lost it,' said Frances scornfully. 'And as for the money missing from the gun-room, I deny that I even knew there was any there until the news of its loss was all over the Court. Search my room. Search my baggage. You will find nothing, except three gold sovereigns in a stocking in the bottom left-hand corner of my work-basket. Those are my savings.'

'Then you must have the bracelet on you,' said Maud. 'I suggest that we go upstairs now, you and I, and prove the matter one way or the other.'

'Agreed!' cried Frances, and was half-way to the door with Maud at her heels before his lordship could haul himself to his feet. Theo leaped to his patient's side to catch the words Lord Broome was trying to say, but by the time he had lifted his head, Frances and Maud had disappeared.

'Stop them,' Lord Broome was saying. 'Frances . . . danger . . . don't trust Maud!'

But by the time Theo had burst through two sets of doors into the Gallery, both women had disappeared.

Frances was too angry to be cautious. The Gallery was dark; the lamp which stood on the centre chest had blown out. She thought nothing of it. A gale was lashing at the windows.

As she stooped to pick up her train prior to mounting the stairs, a cloak descended over her head and shoulders and strong arms lifted her from her feet. She was thrown to the ground with such force that all the breath was knocked out of her. Her hands and feet were tied. She was hoisted over a broad pair of shoulders and jounced down, instead of up, the stairs. Through the cloister they went, and into one of the ground-floor store-rooms. There were several of these on the ground floor of the Court, all giving on to the cloisters. When the muffling cloak was taken from round Frances' head and she was able to breathe freely, the first thing she saw was the wide streak of light which poured from the uncurtained oriel window of the music-room across the grass of the courtyard. She could see this through the open door of the store-room, which she was facing, held in the bear-like hug of a giant of a man.

'Open your mouth, Miss Chard,' said Maud. Frances opened it to scream. A solid ball of what felt and tasted like wood was thrust far back in her mouth, and her jaws forced further and further apart as Maud twisted a screw at the front of the infernal contraption. Frances' tongue was forced down, and her cry strangled.

'Reproduced by one of the workmen for my grandfather's museum of antiquities,' said Maud. 'It is supposed to be a copy of the type of gag used by the Spanish Inquisition, and I'm happy to see that it works. You never know when these old things will come in useful.'

Meakins, the ladies' maid, entered, carrying a bundle of outer clothing which Frances recognised as her own. The door to the courtyard was shut, and a lamp lit and placed on a rough table.

'You understand what is going to happen?' Maud asked Frances. 'You are going to disappear from our lives—or, rather, Meakins is going to stage your disappearance, wearing your clothes—by running off with that delightfully sharp young man Walter Donne. Strip her, Meakins; help her, Lee.'

Meakins was already busy with the fastenings of Frances' bodice. The burly man, now identified as Lee, held Frances' wrists away from her body. She tried to wriggle away from him, but he was too strong for her. She hardly heard what Maud was saying as her black silk dress, petticoat, corsets, shoes and stockings were stripped off her, to leave her standing barefoot in her shift and drawers, with her hair round her shoulders, trembling with fear and cold.

'In a moment or two, when Meakins is ready, I shall return to the music-room with my mother's bracelet in my hand, and announce that I discovered it hidden in a pocket of your petticoat. Actually, that young toad Agnes had stolen it to play with, and was too frightened to confess that she'd got it when its loss was discovered. I found it in her toy-box, but she'll have sense enough to say she discovered it in one of your drawers, by the time I've finished with her.

'I got in touch with Walter as soon as I heard about the incident at Mrs Palfrey's, realising how I could turn your past history to good use. Walter has his instructions and twenty-five guineas; he is to make his excuses to the company while we are gone, and be ready to meet you—or, rather, your substitute—in the cloisters in a few minutes' time. When I return with my mother's bracelet, I shall say that since no actual offence has been committed, I have decided to take a leaf out of Gavin's book and allow you to leave. I shall invite everyone to the oriel window overlooking the cloisters, and ask them to watch you depart. You will run across the lawn into your lover's arms and everyone will see you embrace him, for I have told Walter to be sure to stand in the light from the window.

'At this very moment one of the footmen is bringing down your trunk and bag, and putting them in the trap which Walter hired at the station. You will be driven off beside Walter, with your baggage, and that will be the end of you. Walter will help Meakins tip your luggage into the river by the Long Pool. She will also weight your clothes—the ones she will be wearing in her impersonation of you, I mean—and drop those into the water, too. She has a change of clothing in the trap for herself, and after she has seen your baggage safely disposed of, and Walter has departed, she will return here to assist me in the last and most pleasurable part of the evening's programme. Ready, Meakins?'

Meakins revolved in the lamplight. She was wearing Frances' evening dress with her black winter coat over it. A thick veil had been wound over the small hat on top of her head, obscuring her features.

'Perfect!' cried Maud. 'Wait for me to open the oriel window before you start across the lawn.'

She turned down the lamp. Rain spattered the threshold as Maud opened the door, gathered her skirts and sped away. Meakins took up her position inside the door. Across the courtyard Frances could make out the white shirt-front of a man in evening dress, standing under the cloisters. She lunged forward, and Lee laughed. He dragged her to one of the stone pillars which supported the Oak Gallery above them, and secured her to it.

Walter moved out into the rain, pulling on an overcoat. Frances threw her weight against her bonds again and again. With eyesight dimmed by tears, she watched Meakins glide over the grass into Walter's arms; she saw Walter embrace the woman, and then escort her out of the courtyard.

She fainted.

*   *   *

Lord Broome lay on his bed, motionless. His eyes were open, but he did not see the anxious faces above him. In his mind's eye he was still seeing a slender figure in black glide into the arms of another man.

'Drink this,' urged Theo, holding a sleeping draught to his friend's lips. 'For Christ's sake, man; don't grieve so. She deceived us all. But we all saw her . . . I've never been so taken in by anyone in my whole life.'

Benson was holding a black lace shawl, and tears were running down his cheeks. 'It was all I could find,' he said.

'She's taken everything else.'

Lord Broome turned away from the proffered sleeping draught, and reached out for the shawl. He put it to his cheek, and closed his eyes.

CHAPTER EIGHT

Frances lay drooping in her bonds against the pillar until long after the light thrown from the music-room had gone out, and noises over her head announced that the company had dispersed to their bedrooms. The stable clock struck eleven, and she came to herself, slowly. The man behind her laughed. He had shut the door on to the lawn and turned up the lamp. He was whittling a walking-stick. She looked at him. He was swarthy, black of hair and moustache. He wore moleskin trousers and a thick flannel shirt. On the floor beside him lay an expensive but vulgar checked overcoat. Frances shuddered, thinking that this man had already committed at least one murder.

The house was quiet above and around them. The stable clock struck eleven. In a gust of wind and rain the store-room door opened and two figures slipped in. Both wore cloaks, and one carried a heavy carpet bag.

'It's a nasty night out,' said Maud, throwing back her cloak. 'I don't envy Walter his drive to the station.' She took a bunch of keys from her pocket. 'Lee—clear away those wood shavings; we mustn't leave any traces. Everything has gone splendidly so far. Dr

Green has given Gavin a sleeping draught and Benson is so much put out by the wicked Miss Chard's defection that he's taken a bottle to bed with him. Both of them are snoring their heads off. I've just been up to listen outside their doors. They haven't bothered to set a guard now that Miss Chard has gone. Isn't that perfect? Poor Miss Chard. I think I am almost sorry for you. Gavin's end will be quick and merciful; he won't know a thing about it. But you are going to have plenty of time to repent crossing my path before you die. You know that this used to be an abbey once? Well, if a nun offended in the old days, she was walled up alive and left to die. I have decided that you deserve the same fate.'

Meakins took a roll of bandages out of the carpet bag and began to wind them round Frances' head, binding in her hair, and covering her forehead, cheeks, mouth and neck with thick white folds of cloth.

'You want to know how Gavin will die? I am taking no more chances. I shall go with Lee, this time. I have the key to the dressing-room, just as Gavin guessed. When you have been lodged in your cell, I am going to help Gavin commit suicide. Poor cousin Gavin! What a shock it has been for him to discover that you are false. Naturally, he is prostrated with grief. They had to carry him to bed, did you know that? And he would not speak to anyone, or look at them. I wondered if he'd had a stroke,

218

but Theo—dear, flustered Theo—said no, it was just shock. No one will think it strange when Gavin is found dead tomorrow morning, with his razor open beside him, and his throat cut. A splendid plan, is it not? Hugo will inherit and marry me, and I shall become Lady Broome at last. I suppose Gavin's original Will has to stand, but I am sure I shall be able to make Isabella see the wisdom of sharing some of her money with me.'

A coarse white gown with a deep hood now came out of the carpet bag, and was dropped over Frances' shoulders. She was grateful for its warmth. Meakins pinned the hood over the bandages around Frances' head, letting it overhang her victim's eyes.

'What about the noise?' asked Meakins, as she pulled some heavy, rusty-looking chains from her bag.

'No one will hear anything in this storm,' said Maud. 'But perhaps Lee had better muffle the blows with cloth, just in case.'

Frances was made to sit on the floor with her legs straight out in front of her while her shoulders remained pinioned to the pillar. Lee fitted her bare ankles into heavy metal cuffs and hammered them shut. A short length of chain, no longer than Frances' forearm, connected the cuffs and would restrict her steps when she stood up.

'All from my grandfather's collection,' said Maud. 'Some of them are genuine antiques and have been used for these purposes before. No one cares about such things nowadays. They will never be missed.'

Frances was released from the pillar, but though she tried to fight free, Lee and Meakins were more than strong enough to restrain her. The white gown was pulled down around her, a strong leather belt was set about her waist and buckled at the back; from the front of the belt depended two more short lengths of chain, each of which ended in a metal cuff. It did not take Lee long to hammer these around Frances' wrists. She could not lift her hands, or part them very far.

'I like to think of you suffering as you have made me suffer,' said Maud. 'There is some prayer in the service for the ordination of nuns and priests for preservation from the vanities of the world. I do hope, Miss Chard, that you appreciate going to your death in sackcloth and chains. I wonder how long it will take you to die? Will you pray for Gavin's soul as you wait for death? I imagine you might. Every hour will seem a day, and every day a year to you in your tomb. I had considered leaving a chink in the wall of your cell, so that I could visit you every night to watch your deterioration, but I decided against it. It would not be prudent. Are we ready? Then let us go.'

Frances was half carried and half dragged along the cloisters by Lee. Maud led the way, carrying the lamp and her keys. Meakins brought up the rear with the carpet bag and Lee's things.

Maud stopped by a door set in the tower below Mrs Broome's apartments and unlocked it with a large key, to reveal a flight of steps descending into the earth. Frances twisted round to look at the rain-sodden cloisters, and feel the clean air on her face, and then she was thrown over Lee's shoulder and carried down into the cellar.

'They don't use these particular cellars nowadays,' said Maud, as she led the way across a spider-haunted room. 'They are part of the original monastery buildings, but they're not supposed to be safe, and no one comes here any more. My grandfather did consider having some work done down here, but he was advised that it would cost too much.' She consulted a map drawn on a piece of paper, and led the way through a maze of smaller rooms, each one more damp than the last, until the lamp began to dim and the smell of rotting vegetation grew strong around them.

'A bit near the river, Miss,' muttered Lee, glancing at the fungus which was growing on the ancient brickwork.

Maud turned two more corners and lifted her skirts to enter a narrow, slimy corridor from which the brickwork was beginning to crumble. A little way along she stopped, and held the lamp high. A small room led off the corridor; no more than a cupboard, it was

221

lined with crumbling bricks and decorated with fungi. The roof was low and the floor of beaten earth. A pile of fallen bricks and some large boulders lay beyond, in the corridor, evidence that someone, at some time, had begun to repair the walls and left the job half done.

Frances was thrown into the cell, her feet touching one wall and her shoulders another. From Meakins' bag Lee produced the largest, heaviest and rustiest chain Frances had ever seen. He threaded it through her belt and, driving a large staple between two bricks, tethered her to the wall of the cell.

Frances managed to get her knees beneath her. Involuntarily her hands clasped in prayer. With every movement her chains rattled, dragging at her wrists and ankles. It was piercingly cold. She could not stop shivering.

Maud laughed. She held the lamp high while Meakins and Lee laboured to fill in the narrow entry to the cell. Frances could not reach them. She could not move more than a foot away from the back wall of her cell. She watched helplessly as they piled boulders and bricks together, building a wall knee-high, then waist-high, and finally shoulder-high.

The light in the cell shifted and decreased as the wall grew. It became smaller than the shawl Frances had placed round Lord Broome's shoulders. Then smaller than his maimed hand.

'God be with you,' said Maud. The light

shattered into tiny points as the last bricks were wedged into the wall. Then Frances heard Maud urge the others away, and the light wavered and went out.

*   *   *

The long hours of confinement in the sick-room, her recent ordeal and the cold of the cell undermined Frances' hold on reality. She trembled and her chains shook with her slightest movement. She imagined that she was in bed, awakening from a nightmare, and started up, hitting her head on the roof of her cell. Her chained wrists dragged her down. She prayed disjointedly, while through her overtired mind flickered images of Gavin and Hugo and Theo, and of the red-coated portrait of Richard Broome that hung over the fireplace in the dining-room.

She thought she heard someone crying behind her, and started in fright, her eyes vainly trying to piece the darkness. Rats! she thought, and in another involuntary movement of terror, twisted and backed away from the direction of the imaginary sound. The chains creaked and bruised her wrists. She found she was holding the rusty chain which tethered her to the wall, and dropped it.

'Rusty . . . rusty . . . rusty . . .' someone said, way back inside her head. 'It's very rusty,' someone else said, and she thought it was

223

Benson, sitting beside her, only of course it couldn't be. Her eyes were not giving her reliable service, for there were luminous patches of fungus on the walls and if she allowed herself to imagine things, she would begin to think that there was a little man in brown sitting beside her. He was wringing his hands, just as she was, and saying that she must hurry because the head of the House of Broome was in danger . . . danger . . . danger . . .

'A chain is only as strong as its weakest link,' said Frances to herself. 'And it is quite true that this chain is very rusty and very old, and that Lee couldn't put all his weight behind the blows with which he drove the staple into the wall, because he couldn't stand upright.'

She struggled up into a stooping position, and managed to get her hands round the chain. She pulled and strained, but nothing happened save that the belt creaked around her waist. Then she began to twist the chain. She lay on the slimy floor and somersaulted over and over until the chain was wound tight and she could not move it any more. Then she threw her weight on it, time and again, until at last something gave, and she was precipitated against the wall, bruised and out of breath. She tried to lift her hands, and found they were still attached to their chains. It was the belt around her waist which had burst open, and not the chain. Tears began to wet the edges of the bandages around her head as she went back to her twisting and pulling.

Did the staple move? Her strength was giving out. Oh, God, don't let all this be in vain.

And the chain snapped off near to the wall, and left her weak and trembling in a heap on the floor.

She was free of the staple, but her hands were still tethered to the belt which now hung in front of her, weighted down by the remnant of the chain which had held her close to the wall. She felt around until she had located the uneven texture of the wall the conspirators had built, and began to push and prod at it. She wound the chain round her hands and battered at the wall. A stone fell out into the corridor beyond . . . then another . . . a large section collapsed, and she was crawling out of her cell. She turned left, because she remembered that that was the way she had entered the cell. The floor was slimy, and she slipped and fell and groped her way along the corridor, not daring to think what she should do next, for she had no map to guide her, and no light.

There! She was out of the corridor, and there was nothing but darkness around her. She did not know which way to go. She lifted her face and prayed, and her prayer was answered, for cool on her skin came the faintest of chills—a breath of fresh air. She did not imagine that Maud would have left the cellar door open, for such carelessness was not in Maud's nature, but Frances craved fresh air, and went towards it as fast as she could. She did not count the turns she took, or the number of times she stumbled over the chain which hung between her feet, but at last she found herself in a cellar which was not totally dark. Moonlight was entering by a grating set high up in a wall, way above her head. The rain had stopped, and the sky was clearing. She could even see the new moon, rising over the stable clock. The night air smelled marvellously sweet and clean, but it made her shiver. Her struggle to escape from the cell had warmed her, but now she felt the cold again.

There was no other way out of the cellar, bar the door through which she had come. She did not want to go back into the depths again, which would mean leaving the light and the fresh air. If it had not been for the danger which threatened Lord Broome, she would have sunk to the floor and waited the night out under the grating, and perhaps died of exposure. As it was, she looked around her for some means of attracting attention to her plight. She tried to release herself from the bandages around her head, meaning to cry out for help if she could once remove the gag which held her mouth open. But she could not. Her fingers were bruised and torn and clumsy, and though she did eventually find her way through the bandages to the gag, she could not master the knack of turning the screw to reduce the size of the gag and thus slip it out of her mouth.

'Hurry . . . hurry . . . hurry . . .' someone said. And again, out of the corner of her eye, she thought she saw the little brown man. She looked that way again, and saw only a pile of logs. They had been there a long time, it seemed, for they were covered with soft spiders' webs. She dragged them to the wall under the grating, and began to pile them one on top of the other. Then she clambered up, hampered by her chains, and grasped the grating above her head. The log beneath her right heel slipped and she was left clinging to the grating with both hands, her feet dangling. With heart-stopping slowness, her weight pulled the grating out of its bed. She could not save herself, but fell heavily on to the logs, with the grating on top of her.

Sobbing, she dragged the grating out of the way and once more, but this time more carefully, began to build herself a platform of logs on which she might climb to reach the opening.

The stable clock struck midnight. She was astounded. Was it only an hour ago that Maud had told her how she intended to kill Lord Broome? She must hurry. She hauled herself up into the courtyard and then, clanking more loudly than any ghost, she tripped and stumbled around the cloisters, and climbed the turret stairs to the Oak Gallery. Her ankles were raw, and so were her wrists, her mouth ached, but . . . 'Hurry . . . hurry . . . hurry! Danger . . . danger . . . danger!'

She came to the door of the State Bedroom and found it ajar. No one was on guard outside. There was no one to help her. She grasped the knob of the door and gently pushed it open. Two figures stood by the red-curtained bed with their backs to her. Maud was holding up her lamp so that its rays fell between the drawn curtains of the bed on to the sleeping figure within. Lee was holding back one of the curtains with his left hand, and in the other he held a cut-throat razor.

'That's it!' said his lordship. He spoke not from the bed, but from the high-backed chair near the window. 'Both of you stand perfectly still. Yes, this is a pistol in my hand, and, yes, I can fire it well enough with my right hand if need be. At this range I can hardly miss. Benson! Arling! Theo! You may come out now.'

The man on the bed rose and took the razor from Lee's hand. It was Arling, in one of his master's nightshirts.

'Now,' said his lordship, who could not see Frances from where he stood, 'tell me what you have done with Miss Chard, and no more of that nonsense about her having left with Donne. I admit you had me fooled for a

228

while. Then Benson found Miss Chard's black shawl; did you really think she would leave her only remaining shawl behind if she had gone willingly? After that I began to use my head, and it was not long before I realised that a substitution had taken place. Miss Chard walks with a free-swinging step, totally unlike the boneless glide of the woman who ran off with Donne this evening. Who was it who wore Miss Chard's clothes? And what have you done with her?'

Maud's head turned from side to side, seeking escape. Suddenly she turned and made for the door. She saw Frances, in monk's gown and chains. Her eyes widened. Her mouth distorted with a soundless cry of horror. Her body bent, knees loosening. Sweat stood out on her brow. She pointed at Frances, and her hand wavered. 'The ghost!' she whispered.

'None of that!' said his lordship, sharply. 'Do you think Lee frightened me, dressed up in a white robe? Richard ought to have got his facts right; our family ghost is a small and ancient soul in a brown robe—either an old family retainer from the early days of the Broome occupancy, or a Franciscan monk. I've never seen him, and I doubt if you have, either.'

Maud continued to stare at Frances. Her hand to her mouth, Maud took one step back, and then another, until she was pressed to the cupboard behind her. Two men entered from the dressing-room, holding a sullen Meakins captive between them.

Theo said, 'I caught her sneaking up the stairs in the direction of her bedroom. She's got some odd things in her carpet bag; my uncle's bottle of emetic for one, and some keys, and a hammer. What shall we do with her until the police come?'

'Perhaps she can tell us where Miss Chard is,' said his lordship.

'Police?' quavered Meakins.

'Arling has a groom ready and waiting to send for them. They are staying in the village, you know.'

Maud screamed. She raised both her hands above her head in a gesture of despair and then, realising that she still had hold of the lamps, froze, looking at it. Her face, lit from above, became a mask of fury. Before anyone could stop her, she threw the lamp with all her might straight at his lordship. The lamp broke against the back of the chair on which he was sitting, and flames burst out over the upholstery and over the dressing-gown he was wearing.

Frances thought: This is why I was allowed to escape! Pushing Maud out of the way, she threw herself on Lord Broome, and smothered the flames with her heavy robe and with her hands. His lordship dropped his pistol to help her, while Theo released Meakins to run for the ewer of water from the nightstand in the

230

dressing-room. At that moment Meakins and Lee both made a bid for escape. Arling and Benson fell on Lee, and Theo tripped Meakins as he returned with the water. She fell to the floor in an untidy heap. Maud leaped over her maid, sped through the dressing-room and out into the Gallery.

Frances fainted.

*　　*　　*

In years to come a legend sprang up in the village that Miss Broome had stumbled while crossing the fatal bridge in the park, and been swept away by the swollen river to drown in the Long Pool, like Lilien Jervis. If this was so, it was strange that her body was never recovered. Some had it that she made her way to London, and joined forces with Walter Donne in a life of crime. Once, on a trip to Paris, Mr Manning thought he saw her in a crowd, poorly dressed, and with her hair cropped as if she'd had a fever. He tried to approach her, but if it was indeed Maud whom he had seen, she had no wish to acknowledge the connection, for she had disappeared by the time he reached the spot on which she had been standing, and he never saw her again.

Lee, Jervis and Meakins confessed to the attempts on Lord Broome's life, but placed the blame on Maud as having been the instigator of their crimes. Jervis admitted knowing that Lee had engineered Richard's death, but denied that he had himself been in any way involved. In due course Lee was hanged, and the other two given long prison sentences. Hugo returned to London to look for another job. It was said that he attained some respectable position in the office of a tea importer eventually, but he was never invited to the Court again.

Lord Broome's problems were not resolved with the departure of the conspirators from the scene. Miss Chard's nervous system had been overstrained, and although her burned hands and various grazes responded to Theo's doctoring, her sleep was interrupted by nightmares and at the slightest provocation she would dissolve into tears. In this low state, she brooded on the harsh things Hugo and Maud had said, until it seemed that their judgment must be that of Society. She had always known that she was unworthy to be Lady Broome, and now she became convinced that his lordship's protestations of love were made out of gratitude, and that he would be even more grateful were she now to take her leave of him, so that he might marry some well-born and deserving girl.

Theo visited her every day, dutifully exclaiming over the gifts his lordship had caused to be sent up to her. Each day he asked whether she felt up to seeing his lordship, and each day she cried, and said that she wished she were dead.

'She needs a couple of months' rest at the sea,' said Theo, reporting to Lord Broome. 'She is full of impossible schemes for finding another position as a governess. She is quite unequal to anything like that at the moment, as I pointed out to her. I have suggested that she spend a month in Brighton with a distant cousin of mine, and she is going to think it over.'

His lordship pierced and lit a cigar with great concentration. It took him some time, but Theo did not offer to help. He knew he'd be sworn at if he did. Finally, Lord Broome said, 'Still thinking you can cut me out with her, Theo? Perish the thought. When we are married, I daresay she will fill the house with young people, and you can pick out a nice, prettily-behaved little girl to marry.'

'My lord,' said Theo, becoming very dignified, 'I thought I had made it plain that she did not wish to see you.'

'Oh, yes, I quite understand that a frontal attack is out of the question. She's not eating, you say . . . or sleeping properly. She'd have hysterics if I burst in on her now. You're a pretty good doctor as doctors go, Theo, but you have never understood Miss Chard. I'll tell you what's wrong with her; she's afraid that she will not be accepted by the county when she marries me.'

'Such a marriage would be very unequal.

233

She has no dowry, no friends, no family . . .'

'Precisely. You have at last arrived at an accurate diagnosis of what is wrong with Miss Chard. Can your medicines cure her?'

'No medicine can cure her of wanting the impossible.'

'Then we must supply her with the impossible ourselves, must we not?'

After Theo had left, his lordship smoked his cigar through and then made his dispositions, as if he were planning a military manoeuvre. Letters were sent here and there, as he might once have despatched scouting parties. He drove over to see General and Mrs Armstrong, and negotiated a treaty with them which would not have disgraced a general making peace with a powerful neighbour who might or might not be friendly in the event of a renewal of hostilities. Finally, he informed his battalion— that is to say, his immediate family and the staff of the Court—of his plans, in the event of Miss Chard's departure. A stunned silence greeted his orders, followed by tears on the part of some, and reluctant smiles on the part of others.

The following day Benson brought the letters to his master, instead of Spilkins, who was laid up with shock at hearing his lordship's plans.

'They've started carrying tales to Miss Chard already,' he said, riffling through the letters on the salver before handing them to his master. 'Mr Manning's replied, and Mr Percy Chard from Somerset, and there's three invitations from the Armstrongs and their cronies. I should say you've pulled it off, Major. I mean, my lord.'

Lord Broome overlooked Benson's lack of polish, to slit open the mail and scan the contents. 'So far so good,' he said. 'See that that lot is taken up to the sick-room, will you? Lady Amelia should be there about this time, but if she isn't, will you make sure that she goes there straight away? I'm tempted to take the letters up myself, but I think I'd better not see her until she's digested their contents. I'd like to go out riding, but I'm afraid she might do something foolish like trying to run away while my back's turned. Theo said she was a little stronger today, and talking of leaving at the end of the week.'

'Don't worry, my lord. Her retreat's been cut off. Arling has been gentling a mare for her to ride, and he's ordered the pony cart out, that your late mother used to ride. If she sends down word that she wants the trap to take her to the station, he'll see to it that she doesn't get it before you get back.'

'Good. And, Benson, what I said the other day about pensioning you off . . .'

'Oh, I didn't take no notice of that, my lord. I'm used to your ways by now, and you're used to mine, and what would I be doing living like a lord in London, on a pension?

235

Bored to death, I'd be. I did think maybe I'd be your butler when that fool Spilkins goes to the Dower House with Mrs Broome, but then I thought as it wasn't quite what I've been brought up to . . .'

'You did?' said his lordship faintly.

'. . . and then I thought as I might be your official valet, but that didn't quite suit, either, seeing as I'm not as handy with a needle as I might be . . .'

'It didn't occur to you to wait until I offered you a position?'

'Nah. I've settled in my mind on what would be best for the both of us. Your fac-tot-um, that's what I'm going to be, seeing to bits of business that you can't be bothered to do for yourself. You can build me a bit of a cottage at the back of the stables, next to Arling's place, and I'll be as snug as a bug in a rug.'

'You don't think I can do without you, is that it?'

Benson advised his master to get out into the park while the sun was still shining, and took the letters up to the schoolroom.

*   *   *

Lady Amelia was sitting with Frances—by arrangement with his lordship—when Benson arrived with the letters. Frances was looking very unlike her usual trim self. All her clothes had been ruined by immersion in the Long

236

Pool, and although his lordship had provided her with a trousseau of clothes fit for a princess, she had not felt able to wear any of them. She sat in a chair by the fire, huddled into an old flannel dressing-gown of Nurse's, with her hair in plaits. Benson proffered the letters, told her she was looking peaked and he'd have some nourishing food sent up to her, and withdrew before she could protest that she was not hungry.

She picked up the letters, read them through, looked blankly at Lady Amelia, and said, 'What does he mean by this?' Lady Amelia took the letters out of her hand, read them, and nodded.

'Why, my dear . . . fancy that! Percy Chard is coming to stay. How very pleasant! I remember him when he was in knickerbockers. Why didn't you tell me, you naughty girl, that Percy Chard was your uncle? I see that he's bringing his wife —she was one of the Purbrights, wasn't she?—and two of your cousins with him. Of course. Isabella is to be your chief bridesmaid—I had a word with the bishop about the wedding the other day . . .'

'My uncle and aunt coming here? With my cousins? Does this mean that he wants to acknowledge me now? He refused to do anything for me before. Is it because he thinks Lord Broome wants to marry me?'

'Don't be too hard on him, my dear. It's the way of the world. You must forgive him for his past neglect of you, and ask your two cousins to be bridesmaids. Poor things, I believe they are very plain, but you must remember that they are well-connected. You need not invite them to stay more than once a year when you are married. Now where shall we put everyone? I really think Gavin will have to build another wing, after he's modernised the Court. If we put the Mannings in the . . .'

'I don't understand.' Frances pressed her hands to her forehead. 'Why is Mr Manning bringing his family down here at the same time?'

'Naturally, he is anxious that they make your acquaintance. As you can see from his letter, John is overjoyed that Gavin is about to settle down at last . . . yes, yes . . . and here is the message from your aunt about presenting you at Court. I daresay she will write to you personally in a few days' time.'

'But why should she present me at Court? I am nothing to her.'

Lady Amelia looked faintly embarrassed. 'Because Gavin has asked her to do so, of course. John wants Gavin to go on to some charity committee or other, and . . .'

'. . . so his lordship has bought my presentation at Court by putting some money into one of Mr Manning's charities?' Frances picked up the invitations. 'And Mrs Armstrong and her friends? How have they been won over?'

238

'I don't know. Something to do with a railway that the General is interested in, I think. And, of course, Mrs Armstrong likes to be first with everything. The news of your heroism is all over the county, and it is only natural that she should wish to sponsor your entry into Society. As her protégée, you will be received everywhere.'

Frances burst into tears. 'But, Lady Amelia, I am nobody.'

'My dear!' Lady Amelia patted Frances' head. 'You are the girl Gavin wants to marry. He won't rest, and he won't let anyone else rest, until he has you. I must say he could have done a lot worse. You have breeding, and are well-educated; also, you are not frightened of him, which most young girls are.'

Frances sought for a handkerchief. 'How has he won you over?'

'He did not have to. After what you did for him, I was quite willing to welcome you into the family. Well, just between ourselves, it would make me very happy if you would take Isabella off my hands once you are married. I am getting too old to look after such an extremely silly little girl.'

Frances burst out laughing, and what with her tears and her laughter, Lady Amelia wondered whether she ought not to send for Theo. But at last Frances lay back in her chair.

'Do you really think I ought to marry him?' she asked.

'Yes, my dear, I really think you ought. Your scruples do you credit, but you must admit he has countered them all.'

'By fair means or foul. How much has he paid for me, do you know?'

'That is a question you must ask him yourself, I think.'

Miss Chard considered the matter. 'Of all the underhanded, dictatorial . . . It's bribery and corruption, that's what it is; and I shall tell him so!'

'Yes, my dear, you do that,' said Lady Amelia. 'But only consider what will happen to us all, if you refuse him. Poor Milly will be packed off to the Dower House in disgrace, and since she won't be able to keep a carriage on what Gavin proposes to allow her, she will be completely cut off from Society. Whereas, if you stay here, she will have access to some of her old friends, at least. Then there is Agnes: she must go away to school. I don't deny that that will be a good thing for her, but Milly doesn't want her back in the holidays, because she says that Dower House isn't big enough to hold them both. The child would have to stay at school in the holidays, and her pony would be sold, and she'd be utterly miserable.'

'I should hate Agnes to be miserable,' murmured Miss Chard.

'And Gavin swears that if you go, he will shut up the house and tour the Middle East, which means that the servants will be put on

240

board wages and many of them—especially the younger ones—will leave to seek posts elsewhere.'

Miss Chard nodded. 'His lordship knows I wouldn't like to see Polly and Abel suffer.'

'I don't think he's forgotten anybody, do you?'

Frances smiled, and agreed. Benson arrived with a tray loaded with food, and stood over Miss Chard until she had eaten some of it. Then she went to bed and slept, and slept, and slept, undisturbed by nightmares.

The following morning Agnes knocked on Miss Chard's door. Frances welcomed her, saying that she was just in time to help choose which of the new dresses should have an airing.

'You are going downstairs?' Agnes tore to the door and shouted for Polly, to come to help Miss Chard dress. Then Agnes rushed back into the schoolroom and hugged her governess.

'Steady!' cried Frances, laughing. 'I'm still very shaky on my feet.'

The word spread through the Court that Miss Chard was dressing and proposed to come downstairs in less time than it took her to decide which frock to wear. Lord Broome heard the news and abandoned his papers to change from one perfectly good suit into another, which he thought made him look less like a soldier in civilian clothes. The ladies of the Court practised welcoming smiles, the servants flew around with dusters, and the head gardener anxiously refurbished the flowers in the reception-rooms.

Frances came down the turret stairs slowly. Her legs trembled with the strain, and she had to hold on to the stonework to keep her balance. Agnes and Polly hovered around her, but in spite of their efforts Frances stumbled on the last step, and almost fell.

A wild-eyed man flew down the Gallery and thrust Agnes and Polly aside to take Frances in his arms. 'Idiots!' he said to Agnes and Polly. 'What do you mean by letting her try those stairs by herself? Has nobody around here any sense except myself?'

Frances put her hand over his mouth. 'It's all right,' she whispered. She was crying, but this time for joy.

'Is it?' The fierceness left his expression. He allowed her to stand upright. He ran his hands over the soft blue silk of her bodice, and hugged her till she protested.

'Truly, I am not hurt, my lord. I can stand by myself.'

'Not till you agree to marry me. Say yes, and I'll put you down.'

'Yes, my lord.'

'You only call me by my title because you know it annoys me. Say it properly!'

'Say what?' But the downward sweep of her eyelashes and a fleeting smile betrayed the fact that she knew perfectly what he wanted her to say.

He shook her, but remembering her weakness, did it gently. 'Call me by my own name.'

She hesitated, and then went into his arms. 'Yes, Gavin.' His lordship kissed her, and if there was more of triumph than tenderness in his kiss, be sure that Frances did not object.

'Ah!' sighed Agnes and Polly, as one.

'I knew you'd see it my way in the end,' said his lordship, and bore Miss Chard off to be congratulated by his family.

Chivers Large Print Direct

If you have enjoyed this Large Print book and would like to build up your own collection of Large Print books and have them delivered direct to your door, please contact **Chivers Large Print Direct**.

Chivers Large Print Direct offers you a full service:

☆ **Created to support your local library**

☆ **Delivery direct to your door**

☆ **Easy-to-read type and attractively bound**

☆ **The very best authors**

☆ **Special low prices**

For further details either call Customer Services on 01225 443400 or write to us at

Chivers Large Print Direct
FREEPOST (BA 1686/1)
Bath
BA1 3QZ